I0761399

Slow Stories

Slow Stories

Bette A.

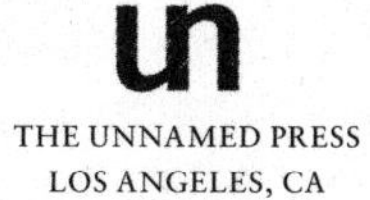

THE UNNAMED PRESS
LOS ANGELES, CA

AN UNNAMED PRESS BOOK

Published in North America by the Unnamed Press.

www.unnamedpress.com

Unnamed Press, and the colophon, are registered trademarks of Unnamed Media LLC.

Hardcover ISBN: 978-1-961884-72-4
EBook ISBN: 978-1-961884-71-7
For Library of Congress and LCCN information, please search their catalogue at www.search.catalog.loc.gov

Cover painting by Bette A.
Cover design and typeset by Jaya Nicely

Manufactured in the United States of America

Distributed by Publishers Group West

First Edition

Contents

Slow Stories

The God in the Box

A GIANT SQUARE BOX appeared on a hill near the edge of a city. It was as high as a small tree, or as high as two people standing on each other's shoulders. The box had no opening, and it seemed to be made from a kind of aluminum.

There is a God in the box, said the people of the city.

They gathered around the box, joined hands, and wished for this God, who had suddenly come upon them, to be a good God.

Thankfully, this appeared to be the case. Soon, a peaceful feeling spread throughout the city.

The people began to bring gifts to the box. They planted fruit trees and flowers around it. On Saturdays, they cleaned the box carefully with water they carried up from the river. On Tuesdays, they sang to it. When someone was grieving, they knelt by the box, and their pain eased a little.

Over the years, the story was passed down: the God had come, they had wished it was good, and it turned out that it was.

Then one day, a person asked, "What if the God became good only because we wished it to be? What if it is shaped by our wishes?"

This was a dangerous question. Immediately everyone became scared of their own desires. Soon, new wishes began manifesting themselves. There was no way to prove it, and no one would admit to wishing such things, and yet terrible things began to happen. Stealing and slander, abuse, hostility and murder. Everywhere, there was widespread suspicion. The God in the box had become cruel, and everyone was imprisoned by dark desires.

In the following period, the people in the city trained themselves to suppress their wishes. They lived and worked in a kind of meditation state, bereft of desire. No one looked to the box anymore, and it was slowly covered by moss and leaves.

Then one day, a child, staring out his classroom window at school, had a thought. "Maybe I can change things not by wishing but by doing," this child thought. "Doing tiny little things that are hardly noticeable." That evening, he climbed up the hill to the box and peeled a mandarin while sitting next to it. He peeled it with utmost attention, studying the membrane that held the bright orange moisture containers in place, and ate it slowly and deliberately. When he had finished eating it, he poured some water from his bottle near the roots of the mandarin tree. All the while he was doing these things, he thought of the God in the box.

The next day, when the child greeted people in the streets, he did it with the same kind of dedicated attention. Curious and open, he looked into people's eyes, taking several moments to see them. And again, he thought of the God in the box while he did it.

And he could see it working. The God in the box was changing ever so slightly. The people in the city began opening their eyes a little wider. They started feeling care and curiosity again when their eyes locked with someone else's in the street.

The children in the boy's class changed too. They became louder and wilder. They brought pine cones from the forest into the classroom, saying, "Look at how this is, *look*!"

The boy told his teacher about it, who in turn told some others. Soon, everyone began influencing the God in the box through this new sideways method. And they were rewarded by the God, who brought more and more kindness, care, and attention upon them.

And so the God in the box was shaped in this new way, and in turn, the God shaped the city. Why the box with the God in it had arrived, no one knew, and how it arrived, they did not know either. One day it had just appeared on the hill at the edge of the city—a giant box, as high as a small tree, or two people standing on each other's shoulders, made from a kind of aluminum.

The Stone of Green and Gold

SOMEONE WAS ABOUT to be born into our world.

For the moment, this Someone was still in the Before World (also known as the Afterworld, the Cosmic Egg, the Unified Whole, the infinite, or the Akhashic field). It looks a bit like a lake. It is not a lake, but it looks a bit like one. From this lake this Someone emerged, ready to choose a life to be born into. It could choose a life long or short, full of new things or a repetition of a previous life; it could be a whale or worm or person or bird.

This particular Someone was very stubborn. It had been a very stubborn tree, a very stubborn rat, a very stubborn moss, a very stubborn human, and many other stubborn life-forms.

Right now, it was considering being born once again into a human life.

This Someone remembered all its previous lives as human. It had spent most of these lives in constant fear of pain. Instead of living the life in all its potential, it had started to walk a very narrow path of avoidance, which had caused it to die before actual death took place. It was only when this Someone returned from its human life into the Before World that it remembered why there was no need for fear.

This time, this Someone decided to take that understanding with it. And as it transferred from the collective to the individual, or from superposition to a definite state, or however you want to call it, it repeated to itself one thought. It repeated this one thought over and over again, it held on to this thought very tightly, it held on to it with all its might as it was submerged in forgetting and came out of a mother into the world—our world, on the earth, in the here and now.

"The child is holding on to something," said the midwife who helped deliver the baby.

She looked at the little clenched fist of the baby girl she had just helped into the world. Babies are often born with their hands clenched—that was normal—but this time she saw something shiny in the baby girl's left hand. She carefully unfolded the tiny fingers. In her little hand, the girl was holding what looked like a small stone. A pebble. It was part shimmering gold, part pale green. The two shades intertwined like entangled snakes.

In all four decades as a midwife she had only twice seen a baby be born with a token from the Before World. One time she delivered a boy who was born with the name of his father inscribed on his tongue, and one time she delivered a girl with a feather in her armpit.

The midwife told the parents about the stone in a hushed voice. The parents cried, and the mother took the baby from the midwife's arms and held her tightly, turning away from her. The midwife understood. In their country it was not seen as a good sign to be born with something from the Before World. Children like that were known to be stubborn, and they were often blamed when something went wrong, like the girl with the feather, who was hanged when the grape harvest was devoured by birds.

The parents chose to give the stone to the midwife and asked her to never speak of it to anyone. They named the child Nini, the lightest name they could think of, and not stubborn at all.

Nini had a joyful childhood. Her parents were kind and interested in her, and she often went foraging in the forest with her father, who patiently told her all the names of things. Nini had a remarkable memory, and she loved knowing what everything was called and how everything worked, a curiosity her father happily indulged. After their long days of walking in the forest, she often felt as though the forest remained inside her, and she could feel the dark, tall trees making dark, tall shadows inside of her. She felt the same when she looked at the clouds: she could simply feel them passing through her chest as they passed through the sky.

Nini's mother was a very strict but warm woman. She never had any patience for Nini's stubborn insistence on knowing every detail about everything, but she held Nini tightly in her big, warm arms for several minutes every morning and told her poems and stories before she went to sleep. Nini slept in a single bed with her parents, with her dog, Solex, at the foot of it. Nini knew very little pain or struggle in these young years. Her first experience of pain came when she was ten and Solex died, and her parents had to console her for weeks on end. But Nini discovered that when she ran through the woods, it still felt as if Solex were running with her. This gave her joy, to know that Solex, though no longer outside of her, was still inside of her, and so, she thought, she must still be inside of Solex as well. She did not question this, just accepted it as a fact, as children do with all new things they discover.

Then a war came to the country. Cities, towns, and villages were all invaded by soldiers from a neighboring country. Bombs dropped. Everywhere, it seemed, apartment buildings and houses were on fire or crumbling. When Nini saw the soldiers walking up the path from the bottom of the mountain in the early morning, she ran into the bedroom and warned her parents. Her mother quickly hid Nini in the small space behind the closet in the bedroom, where her father kept his hunting gun. The space was very narrow, and Nini had to stand upright with her head turned to the side to fit. Her mother placed the sideboard back against the closet as her father tried to speak with the soldiers who had arrived at the door. They both heard her father yell in the front room, a deep cry of protest, and then a bang. Nini stubbornly tried to break free from behind the closet, pushing the sideboard away. She begged her mother to hide in there with her, though she knew there was no room.

"Quiet," her mother chided, smacking Nini out of her hysteria into silence. Quickly, she closed off the hiding place again and turned around, aiming the hunting gun at the door to face the soldiers. Nini heard a bang, then silence. She heard a falling sound and her mother speak in a soft voice, pleading. She heard the soldiers laugh and yell for some time, her mother screaming, and then she heard a bang, another bang, another bang.

One day later Nini was let out of her hiding place by the midwife. The midwife had kept the soldiers away from her home by the mountain's edge by creating a repellent scent, made by burning sulfur in oil. No one in their tiny little town had survived the invasion, except for the herder, who had been out in the far fields, and two four-year-old children, twins, who had been hiding under their father's boat. The soldiers had moved on to the next town, where they continued their rampage. Nini moved in with the midwife, together with the two young children, and she grew from a childish twelve-year-old into a very old thirteen-year-old. And she became something like an older sister to the two young ones, who were called Isa and Jin.

When Nini was sixteen, the midwife, who was old, asked Nini to sit with her.

"You must know," she whispered.

"Know what?" Nini asked.

"You were born with something unusual. A stone of two colors. You brought it with you from the Before World. I hid it in the ground, in a box behind the shed, where I keep the buckets and the rakes. We thought it would be bad luck, but you have had bad luck even though I took it from you—too much bad luck!—so you may as well have it and know this about yourself. Dig it up when I am dead."

Nini dug up the box the morning after the midwife died. She held the little stone in the palm of her hand and looked at the intertwining colors. The sickly pale green and the shimmering gold. Instantly she became aware of a memory that existed somewhere in the back of her mind. In fact, it was not really a memory, it was in between a feeling and an idea, something she did not understand but at the same time knew very well. It was just a little too far away to grab it.

In the following nights, Nini stared at the stone before falling asleep, trying to understand its meaning. It occurred to her that the stone, with its ugly and beautiful sections, was similar to her life. The golden joyful years versus the pale horror years, the warm love she had felt emanating from her parents versus the cold hatred she felt from the soldiers, the blissful lightness of her childhood versus the sickening nightmares that she had now, that were taking over her. She called the golden parts of the stone "Joy" and the dark parts "Pain."

Nini braided a little pocket for the stone and wore it around her neck. She wore it as a reminder of what she had decided: she was going to make the lives of the twins fully golden. She was going to manufacture joy for them and keep any pain at bay. She often felt anger at her parents for not protecting her—if they had foreseen the trouble, if they had listened to warnings, if they had constructed a larger shelter, they could have kept all of them safe. And if she hadn't looked out the window that morning, she would also have been dead.

It became Nini's sole mission to make sure Isa and Jin were protected. She forbade them to go out after dark, to talk to strangers, and she went into town every day to get information about the wars that were raging in other countries and might spill over into theirs. Nini dug a large hole under the shed and built a shelter for the three of them, filling it with jars of salted food and dried fruit. She excavated a secret passageway from the shelter to the well, and she set up traps on the path from the bottom of the hill to their house, so any intruders would be noticed and distracted.

She also made sure to take care of the joy in their lives: she made toys for Isa and Jin, she sang with them, she ran with them through the woods, she held them close when they felt alone, she did not let any sad feeling linger on their faces.

When Nini saw the children play together in the forest, she was simultaneously filled with a deep love and appreciation for the children, a sadness at the innocence that she herself had lost, and an ever-increasing fear of hurt happening again. In all the country there was no one who took better care of their children than Nini, who listened to the sound of each breath they took, tasted each mushroom they foraged, taught them how to stand up for themselves, how to run, how to detect a brewing storm.

When Jin and Isa were seventeen, they came into their mother's room one night—they called her "Mother" now—to talk. They said they were grown and ready to go. They thanked her profusely for everything she had done, they kissed her hands, and they cried. The next morning they left for the city, promising to visit often.

Nini was left alone in a dark, empty house, with no way to see what the children were doing, what was happening to them, or whom they were talking to. The pale green feeling she had been trying to keep away now entered her world fully, taking up every space in her mind, taking up every room in her house, filling her with images and sounds that combined horror memories of her parents' murder with visions of terrible things that might happen to Isa and Jin. She tried to calm herself by working on the shelter, but the fear pulled at her from the inside, sometimes falling silent for one merciful moment, only to rise up stronger and more vicious in the next. Nothing she did could quell these waves.

At night, Nini rolled up into a ball in the corner of the bed, her back pressed against the wall, her face toward the doorway.

Neighbors who stopped by to check on her gave her well-meaning advice. Find a distraction, get a lover, have children of your own.

If this is life, Nini thought in those moments, why would I give it to others?

When the children came back to visit their mother three months later, they found her thin and shaking, sitting by the window that looked out at the road where the soldiers accessed the village during the war. "Please," they said to her, "why don't you go out and forage? Don't you love to feel the wind on your skin when you are out in the fields, hear the way the trees rustle, giving you that fluttering feeling inside? Don't you love to sit by the stream and watch all the drops of water go on a journey, from the top of the mountain along the stones and into the roots of the trees? Please come with us."

But Nini could not do it. The fearful thoughts had seized her mind completely, and she could no longer enjoy anything. All she could do was work on the shelter and try to think of the many ways pain might enter their lives and how to prevent it.

"I have to remain vigilant," she said. Unconsciously she clasped the pocket with the stone on her necklace.

"This is not vigilance," the children said.

When Jin and Isa left in desperation, Nini went outside, tore her necklace from her neck, and took out the stone. She yelled and threw the stone far away from her. It hit the rocky wall of the mountain, tumbled down, and fell into a large crevice, where the mountain split open. Instantly, the crevice became illuminated. Nini stepped toward the illuminated opening in the mountainside. She saw in the distance two children running away from her, one golden, emanating light, the other one pale green, emanating darkness.

Nini followed them farther and farther into the deep cave, without thinking about where she was going or how she would find her way back. The jagged rocks of the crevice gave way to smoother rocks as she got deeper into the cave. She kept her eyes on the illuminated child, who radiated a soft, warm yellow, like the morning sun. Her light shone on the walls of the cave and made the little crystals in the stone sparkle as she skipped lightly through the tunnels. The other child was moving more insecurely and abruptly, staying close to the walls, but never falling far behind. Wherever this darkness child stepped, all light shrank away.

Nini called out to the illuminated child. "Wait," she yelled. "Hold on!" But it wouldn't listen.

Finally, she called the name she had given it: "Joy!"

Instantly, the illuminated child stopped. Nini stepped toward the child and got hold of her arms. She pulled the child toward her. Immediately, the darkness child leaped at them, screaming. Nini pushed her, or it, away. She ran farther down the cave, pressing Joy tightly against her chest, trying to get away from the screaming being behind them. She reached a dead end, where the rocky ceiling met the ground. She found an alcove, in the corner, and pushed a few rocks up against it. Then she crawled into this tiny space, her body cloaking the illuminated child, who seemed smaller now. Nini whispered to her: "I'll keep you away from her."

Outside the darkness child, whom Nini called "Pain" in her mind, howled and raged, unable to get to them. The screams pierced Nini's eardrums. She pulled her knees up and lay on her side with the illuminated child against her chest, who struggled to break free from her arms. For a long time she waited, her arms locked around the child, while outside the yelling and scratching got larger and louder with each passing moment. Slowly, Nini saw the light in her hiding place fade. The child she held was growing dimmer and smaller and thinner in her arms, until she was only a shadow, and then she disappeared altogether.

Alone again, Nini sat up. She did not hear the darkness child anymore either, she had gone too. She heard only the silence that she knew from that day when she was in the hiding place behind the closet, when the soldiers had left. She relived that moment, the aloneness and the darkness, the certainty that she would die. The feeling made her unable to move. She had no idea how much time had passed until she heard someone call her name. She was vaguely aware of a dog barking, of arms curling around her body.

And she lost consciousness.

As she departed from her body, Nini saw a yellow light above her and high towers reaching up toward the light. The towers swayed a little, and she recognized them to be dandelions only when one of the seeds detached and started floating away. Then she rose up. Some enormous strength coming from under her was making her rise up toward the light. "I was once a flower!" she thought. An exhilarated feeling ran through her as she stretched toward the delicious warm light. Other sensations came back to her. The feeling of pulling a mouse apart with her beak. Growling and hissing at something. A strong urge to dig, dig, dig. The memory of gliding through deep, dark, icy water. Her hand, hairy and big, pulling the trigger of a cold gun.

And she remembered the Before World. How the lake, or what looked like a lake, shifted into different shades, forms, and compositions, where everything was in everything all at once, nothing more was ever created, and nothing was ever lost. The thought she had grabbed on to, the thought that formed into a stone, came back to her too.

Nini opened her eyes.

She was lying in bed in her house by the mountain. Jin was asleep in the chair in the corner. He had put a glass of water next to her, and her stone was next to it, on top of the broken necklace, which she had ripped from her neck in the garden.

Nini could hear the wind picking up outside. She looked up to the sky through the window. A round moon yellowed the fast-moving clouds. She felt the clouds move through her, like she had when she was a child. She stayed very still like this, watching the sky, until the sun rose. She felt the rays warm her as they came in through the window, and she could feel herself inside the rays, and the rays inside her, the scorching, furious, raging sun inside her, burning everything to the ground and letting everything grow. She remembered Solex, how she had felt him inside of her when he was gone.

Jin opened his eyes.

"Hello, Jin," Nini said. "Thanks for bringing me back from that cave."

Jin was quiet for a moment, staring at her. Then he stood up and burst out into relieved laughter, so clearly had the fear departed her voice. Isa came in from the other room. She too started laughing.

The next day, the children returned to their lives in the city. Nini returned to her life too, and she expanded it, making a flower bed in the garden and accepting a lover. She still reinforced the shelter after each rainfall, processed jars of preserves, and dried and salted meats for winter. She braided blankets for Isa when she suffered a stillbirth and grew very quiet, and she saved up money for Jin, who had received a call to join the army and had not been heard from since.

Nini cried more, not less, than before. She went into town more often and talked to people. If you ever go there, you will see her. She often sits by the bridge over the river, sometimes tossing a stone in the air. When people are in pain they are told to go see her, so she can help them, but she does nothing in particular to help them. She just sits there while they cry and talk, and in her stillness, sometimes something muddled grows clear.

The Endless House

1.

A GIRL WAS BORN. She was born in a small house in a village in a desert. Just like all the other houses in this village, this house consisted of one room only, at least that's the way it was before the baby was born. After the baby's first night, a new door appeared in the house. Behind that door was a new room. The room was dark and red and empty, with a low ceiling and rounded corners. It was impossible to enter the room. When the mother tried to step through the doorway, it was as if she was blocked by an invisible wall.

Outside the house, the people of the village gathered to examine the strange addition to the building. The walls of the new room were made from a kind of mirrored glass that did not break, no matter how hard the villagers tried. They threw bricks at the walls, tried to smash them with sledgehammers and pickaxes and nasty looks.

Not so much as a crack.

The villagers decided the best thing to do was to pretend the new room wasn't there, because nobody understood why and how the room had appeared, and if you thought about it—really, really thought about it—it was more likely that the room wasn't there at all. They were people of the desert, after all, and they were accustomed to mirages.

Six months later, after a hot and dry summer night, it happened again. Another door and another room appeared. This new room was a small white cubicle, and again, no one could enter it.

When some villagers came inside the little house to look at the new room, one of the village boys took the baby from the crib and held her up in front of the doorway of the new room. The baby, named Elvira, reached out her little arms and touched the doorframe and the wall inside the room, something none of the villagers had been able to do.

Immediately, the villagers started whispering among themselves: "The baby's got something to do with it . . ."

The mother started crying. She pulled her baby from the boy's hands and chased all the villagers out of her house.

After analyzing the situation, the villagers came to one conclusion: "The baby has dreamed the rooms into being."

They gathered outside the house and shouted at the mother through the front door: "The best solution—the best solution would be to bring the baby to another village and let them deal with it."

The mother did not want to hear any of it and refused everyone entrance to her house. From that moment on, the mother and the baby lived together, excluded by the other people in the village. The only one who still came to visit was Elvira's grandmother, who'd sit in a corner of the room ticking her knitting needles together, making scarves and blankets for the little one.

Weeks and months and years went by, and rooms kept appearing; at one point a new room came into being every other week. The people in the village tried to ignore it, but the house grew closer and closer to their houses, and when one of the new rooms squashed a chicken coop, they borrowed a large crane in the city, lifted the house from the ground with the mother and the child inside, and drove it four days into the desert, where they left it.

2.

The mother stayed in the house with the child Elvira. Close to the house was an oasis, a sheltered bit of fertile land by a shallow river, where she created a vegetable patch. Traveling merchants often stopped there to set up camp. From these merchants the mother got meat and flour, and in return she allowed them to see inside the house, pointing out all the doors and all the rooms behind them.

For a while, everything was fine. The baby grew up to be a sweet child who liked to talk and dance, and watched hours and hours of ballet shows on the small black-and-white TV they got from one of the merchants. She helped her mother make dough and soup.

The only thing Elvira did not like was leaving the house. When she got too big for her mother to carry, she refused to leave the house altogether. She clung to door handles and screamed, while her mother pulled at her legs, begging her to come into the fresh air.

From the moment she started walking, she started to disappear. She wandered into the new corridors and rooms of the house where her mother couldn't follow her, and she stayed away for hours.

Meanwhile the house kept growing. It was hard to see the outline from outside, because the walls were all made from that same mirrored glass the first room was made of, and it reflected its surroundings. From the front, only the original door was still visible.

Endless halls, floors, and entire wings had grown on to the house. The mother could swear she heard sounds coming from the rooms sometimes. Now and then when a door was open, the mother thought she saw a dark figure move through the hallways. The girl told strange stories when she came back from her journeys through the house. She described people the mother had never met and events that should not be possible.

One night, when the girl had once again been missing for days after she disappeared into one of the wings of the house, the mother desperately called "Elvira, Elvira" into the open doors. Suddenly she saw an old woman in one of the hallways, walking toward her. The woman looked up from her knitting, and instantly the mother recognized the grandmother they had left behind in the village. Her knitting needles continued clicking together as she walked. The mother staggered back and yelled: “I want out of this hell house.”

That night the mother woke up to a deep scratching sound. When she opened her eyes she saw a new floor sliding out of the ground, by the front door. Without thinking, she jumped up from the bed and ran out the front door, into the desert. A new room grew against the front door of the house, forever closing it off.

3.

The girl Elvira was on her own now. The house consisted of so many rooms it had probably become the biggest house on the planet, and the people in the villages at the edge of the desert called it the “Endless House.” During the first few months, the mother came back every few days to put food and water outside the walls and to shout “sorry” at the building, but after a while she became convinced it was pointless. The child was locked in without food and drink. She must have died.

Still, the house seemed to keep on growing. Once in a while, inhabitants of neighboring villages boarded a tour bus to travel to the house and take pictures. But the glass walls reflected the clouds and the sand, so it was hard to find, and when they did find it, it was hard to get a good picture. After a while most people stopped believing in the house and it became a story, like so many stories about people who can make things fly with their eyes, people who have four legs and two heads, people who come back from death.

4.

Many years later—seventeen years later, to be precise—a young tour guide accidentally drove his Jeep into one of the walls of the house. He was looking for a sheltered place to set up camp for tourists from colder countries, who were willing to pay good money to sleep in a tent in the desert.

The boy was driving slowly and only grazed the building. When he got out of the car to find out what happened, he saw the contours of the house. "This has to be the Endless House," he thought, "the house of the girl Elvira." People had told him stories about it, unbelievable stories, like the ones about birds made of flames and people being born from the rib of someone else.

He immediately wondered how he could make money from having found this house; he imagined bringing the tourists there. But those thoughts came to a halt when he noticed the shape of a girl on the other side of the glass wall. She had long, wild hair, and she was wearing a knitted dress. She raised her hand and smiled at him. He put his hand on the glass wall, but she turned around and disappeared.

From this moment on, the young man returned to the house every day and drove around the building in his Jeep, hoping to see her. She was stuck in his thoughts. Not because she was more beautiful than other girls—he'd had the most beautiful tourists in his tent—but because she was a dream, a myth. After weeks of driving around the house without seeing a glimpse of her, he desperately yelled at the mirrored walls: "Elvira! Let me in! I want to see your rooms! I want to see you! Let me in!"

That night the boy woke up in his own bedroom with the girl from the Endless House standing next to him. Behind her other people were standing, strangers, some of them wearing uniforms; others wore ballet clothes or merchant clothing.

"Welcome," Elvira said.

The boy got up from his bed and followed her out of his room. Instead of the door to his parents' room that he always saw across from his, he saw a long, high corridor with an enormous amount of doors.

"Am I dreaming this?" he asked the girl.

"What do you mean?"

"Is this real, or am I dreaming this?"

"I don't understand what you mean," she said. She took him by his arm and led him into a large chamber. They danced over the black-and-white checkered floor while an orchestra played a tune from a popular soap opera. Ballet dancers dressed as swans listlessly performed a dying scene.

The girl clung to him while they spun in the corners, and she raised her feet from the floor. By the end of the dance she hung from his neck like a monkey, her legs wrapped around his waist.

"I don't know who these people are," she whispered in his ear, nodding at the other dancers, who smiled at him. "I am afraid of my own house. I don't know who lives here anymore."

The boy felt smothered by her, and he wanted to get out of there. He pushed her away and ran down the corridor, back to his bedroom, where he lay down on the bed. Just like in every other story, he would now wake up in his own house. He relied on that.

But it did not happen.

He slept, and he woke up in his bed in his bedroom, but outside his bedroom door there was still the long, high corridor of the Endless House instead of his parents' bedroom.

An elderly woman sat in a corner of his bedroom holding knitting needles, she was clicking them against each other, a long scarf covering her lap. She smiled at him.

5.

"I want out!" the boy shouted, running down the corridors.

The girl Elvira emerged from one of the rooms and took his hand. She led him down two stairs, through a long hallway, and across one completely dark room, to one of the building's most outer walls.

"You are out," she said, pointing at the window.

He saw himself outside, walking back and forth on the other side of the glass wall. The Jeep was parked behind him. In the distance he heard his own voice shouting: "Elvira!"

"Am I here, or am I there?" he asked the girl.

"That depends from which side you're looking," she said.

He watched the other him outside the house walk back to the Jeep and climb in, the headlights lighting up.

"Which one am I?" he said as he watched himself drive away in his car. "Which one is me?"

He grabbed her by her shoulder. The endless corridors around him seemed threatening now. People stared at him from different rooms and corners.

"Can I get out?" he asked Elvira.

She smiled, but didn't answer, and walked away from him, her hand sliding over the smooth glass wall.

Memorial

HERE TOO THEY HAVE FALLEN, like you will fall one day.

Twenty-four people we remember here at this memorial.

If you look closely you might find bones or a tooth, or a piece of a knife that you can take home with you.

These twenty-four remains were found on a sunny morning, a long time ago. The bodies were preserved by the cold earth of the bog. Some were found with a contorted expression on their faces—those were the ones who were defeated right in the midst of battle, delivering blows. Then there were those who were found with a tired look on their faces. These were the ones who had to endure most when the battle was already over, and they collapsed from exhaustion onto the soil.

The silver bits and pieces you can see here and there in the grass, the shards reflecting the sunlight, these are bits of their harnesses, torn apart. Intact armor was found too, still on the bodies of those defeated. This armor was made too heavy by their owners, making it hard for them to move and forcing them to watch, frozen, as the battle raged on. These persons were defeated from within.

And then there was one person, a young man, who was found with a look on his face like no other. He had his eyes half open, and his mouth was turned up in a smile. There were no knives found around him, no armor. There was no sign of terror on his face. Just that vague smile.

You might think he was stabbed in the back and he went down before he realized what was happening, but no, his back was undamaged. There was only one puncture wound on this young man's body. It was right in the middle of his chest, between his outspread arms. In his right hand he was holding a wooden flute.

This young man, this Ramses, as he was called, had never armed himself. When his peers began forging knives and axes and welding metal for their chain mail, Ramses spent all his time carving wooden flutes.

He was warned: "The battle will come. You won't last a minute, you won't survive the first blow, if you don't arm yourself. The battle comes for everyone, so it will come for you too."

But Ramses just said, "Maybe it will, maybe it won't. I'll see it when it happens."

Ramses wouldn't even listen to his own father, who had commanded Ramses to arm himself. His father had never been a very persuasive man. When he ordered his son to do things, he could not help but smile or give his son a little playful push. And so the boy did not take his father seriously. He did not take anything seriously. This was not surprising to the father, who had very carefree tendencies himself, and his wife had a very distracted nature. Knowing that they were passing these combined soft qualities on to their child, they had given their son a strong name. Ramses. It did not help.

The other villagers asked Ramses if he thought of himself as worthless, since he did not arm himself. They told him horrific stories about battle, the different forms it could take. Not a day went by without someone recounting to Ramses the terrifying ordeal a grandfather had endured or the pain a great-uncle had gone through; not a day went by without someone telling Ramses of the horror awaiting him for not properly arming himself. Some of the villagers even went as far as punching Ramses whenever he walked by, for his own good, so he would understand what pain was and be inspired to vigilance. But no one was willing to hit him very hard, because Ramses was an agreeable guy and he made nice flutes.

In the end, of course, the villagers were right. When the battle came Ramses was the first to fall. He probably did not even recognize the battle when it came for him, considering the stupid smile that remained on his face.

The other villagers fought.

Most of them endured for years, decades. Sometimes, when the battle calmed down for a moment, they thought of Ramses, and they wished they could grab him by his shoulders and say, “See, we told you so!” Because in some way it bothered them that Ramses had died obliviously, not knowing what hit him and carefree till the end.

Here at this memorial, at least, no one can deny the battle. If ever again there is someone as stupid as Ramses, he can be taken here, and he can see with his own eyes the bones and the skulls and how the harnesses were ripped apart.

In any case, twenty-four persons we remember here: twenty-three brave ones, and Ramses.

Virtually Everything

WHAT WE KNOW is that we got born.

What we know is that we are in the mirror house.

What we know is that there are at least 405 of us—we have counted by shouting our number in succession from all corners of the house. Of course, a voice might be too far or still be on its way to us.

We know that we are at least 405 voices, but we are many more bodies. The mirrors that cover each surface in the house duplicate us. They send our reflections around at the speed of light.

What we know is the speed of light. We know that the mirrors reflect only a part of us and some light gets lost, which is why we are so green and vague.

My name is dot-a-dot-dot-dot-r. I got born to our mother in the reception room. Our father was there too. I have not seen it with my own eyes, but some of the others told me they remember when I got born. Some said they were worried how red I was when I got born, and others said they thought I looked like a fish. This is contradictory, so at least one of these statements is untrue.

One day you got born. My little sister, dot-lain.

Before you, dot-lain, I played during the day.

What we like to do is to play in the mirrors. We stretch out our arms in front and let our reflected hands touch. It is so fun to see yourself many times above and below you! It is so exciting to be distorted and stretched!

We have virtually everything here. We grow potatoes and cucumbers, they grow like weeds. We also grow weeds. There are chickens here, they are terribly dirty. We have one mother, and she is lost. We are sure we will find her one day, but in the meantime we have her reflection.

The mirrors took up my entire mind before you, dot-lain.

It was hard for us to think beyond them, and why would we? For us it was fine to see in reflections, but, dot-lain, you wanted to look at my actual face. You told me to look down at my actual feet, you asked me to close my eyes and sense inside me.

Dot-lain, it was you who made me look at myself. I found out that from my own eyes, when I look down, my body looks like this. Or like this. Or like this.

"I do not dream of mirrors," you said to me. "At night I dream of the bark of a tree and I rub my face against it." Your eyes took on a wild delight, a look that I only knew of the times when we thought we had found Mother.

Dot-lain, when you got born you were talking about your legs, how the blood pulsated through them. You once squeezed your flesh until it bruised. I watched you bite your arm until it bled. And you cried, which caused me pain.

"I cannot help that we have lost our mother," I told you. "We are sure we will find her one day."

"I do not want to find our mother, I want to find the way out," you said. And when you started to map all the rooms and the tunnels to find your way out, I wanted to help you. I felt I should care for you because I saw you get born.

Dot-lain, did we not map a big part of the house? Was that not enough? I still remember: this hallway coils into itself, that room is circular, and those pillars, concave. For months our bodies slid over the mirrors. We made marks on them with our tongues, leaving greasy licks that were a thousand times replicated, so we could distinguish where we had already gone.

The first time we made a monthlong circle around a pillar of mirrors it was so funny! I had so many laughs from it! But you did not like it, dot-lain. From then on, you left chicken bones on the floor to mark in which direction we had gone, hoping the others would leave them alone.

Sometimes you tried to scale the mirrored surfaces if you thought you saw a light source above.

"Every light source has to be followed to get to its origin," you said. "It should be getting brighter."

I still do not know why the light would promise an exit for you.

Sometimes you banged on the mirrors, but they would not break. "Are the mirrors shifting?" you yelled into the house. "Are they turning so fast we do not notice it?"

"We do not know," we shouted back.

You and I found out that some mirrors had little holes in them, and when we looked through them we saw closed-off rooms. Sometimes just one lonely reflection bounced around in there. When I saw those I said, "Please, I want to stop," but you kept talking to me, into me, with your voice soft and your mouth all the way pressed on my ear; you talked words into my earhole: "We need to go beyond the mirrors . . . There is something . . . I know there is . . . We'll get out, right right, right, right?"

"Why are you so unhappy when we have virtually everything?" I asked you one night. I was getting older, and I wanted to spend time with my earlier, unwrinkled reflection, like many of us did in old age.

"I am not unhappy," you said.

But you would not get up anymore, remaining on the floor with your eyes closed, slowly fading. Your existence was more defined by the mirrors than ours, I think sometimes now. How you hated the mirrors, making them scratchy with your nails and breathing your reflection away.

Some nights I dream of you. And in those dreams you find a small black door in the ceiling, and I watch you climb up into the sky while I stay behind. The truth is that I would never have followed you even if you had found your exit. I had known for a long time how I got born.

Often I think of your face, dot-lain, when you finally understood about us.

"But how am I interacting with you?" you asked. "How do we let our actual feet touch each other, how do you make your own decisions? Why do you react to me without delay?"

How could we ever have told you? You did not even understand about Mother.

We could only tell you to be very light and to play.

The Rock

On a certain day, a man arrived in a certain village somewhere in the desert. He was carrying a large rock on his shoulders. He was a skinny little man, and the rock was almost as big as he was. The citizens of the village watched the man as he slowly made his way toward the market square, his back hunched and his eyes tired.

"Look." One of the villagers pointed at the man. "He's never once stopped to put that rock down."

"Look, he's eating his bread, and even then he doesn't put it down."

And: "Look, he is leaning against a tree, because of course he's tired, so why the hell won't he put it down?"

The villagers whispered and couldn't stop staring at the man. It was a very unpleasant sight, and it was also inconvenient for them to be so distracted, because they needed to do their grocery shopping. After a short period of whispering and staring, one of the market women had enough and yelled: "Will you put it down already?"

The man raised his head and looked around helplessly. "It's not that I don't want to, you know." His voice was soft and unstable, as if he hadn't spoken in a long time. "I've carried this rock ever since I can remember. Every day and every night. Who knows what will happen when I put it down?"

"Why are you carrying it then?" one villager asked. "What is the reason?"

"I don't know why," the man said. Tears welled in his eyes.

The villagers stared at the flies swarming around him. Looking closer, they could see deep wounds on his shoulders, open and festering.

"I must be sentenced to it," the man said.

The villagers shook their heads. "This can't be right," one said.

"Look at your shoulders, look at your back," another one said. "You're suffering. Just put it down!"

The villagers formed a circle around the man and clapped their hands. "Put it down! Put it down!"

The man twisted his heels nervously in the sand. "I guess I would really . . . I know I would really like to stretch my back. Just once."

The villagers cheered. "Just do it! Put the rock down!"

Hesitantly, the man put his hands on the rock, inched it up slightly, and, with a soft scream, lowered it back on his shoulders again. "I can't!" he said. "Or can I?" Like a scared animal, the man paced back and forth within the circle the villagers had formed around him. The shifting of the rock had revealed a large indent in his spine.

"Come on, do it!" the villagers urged him, looking appalled at the dent in his back.

Suddenly, the man stood still. With shaking hands, he grabbed the rock, lifted it up from his back, and placed it on a heap of sand with a sob. Then he lay down in the sand, and, vertebra by vertebra, he straightened his spine. Tears of joy streamed down his face.

He started to speak. "This day," he said . . .

Unfortunately, we will never know what it was with that day. At that moment, the rock rolled down and smashed the little man's head. The disappointed villagers went silent. They dragged the man's crooked body to the edge of the town, where they left it for the vultures, and they went back to their business.

The Big One and the Small One

THERE WERE TWO HERE, a big one and a small one. There was rain here and there was a shelter. The dry space in the shelter was just big enough for one.

"You must take the dry space," the big one said, "because you are small."

"No, you should," the small one said, because they loved each other.

"The rain is terrible," the big one said. "It slowly takes possession of your clothes, then it goes into your skin and your body, and finally it goes into the bones and never goes out of them again. I can stand it, but a small one like you?"

And so the little one went into the shelter. The rain came down on the big one, and slowly it went into the bones.

"Why is there no one to protect me?" the big one thought. "Why isn't there a bigger one?"

The small one thought of the rain and was angry and scared. Angry because the big one was in the rain and the little one dry and warm. Angry because there was no smaller one who could lie in the small one's protection. And scared because the big one could go one day, and the rain would come down on the small one and go into the bones. The small one was scared that he wouldn't be able to stand it, as the big one had said.

"I'll always be the small one," he thought.

The Other Village

When she was nine years old, the girl saw the other village for the first time. It was on top of the mountain beyond the row of hills that surrounded her own village. Most of the time that mountain was shrouded in a thick layer of mist. But one day—when she was exploring the village cemetery with her younger sister, seeking animal bones for their collection—the sun shone so brightly the entire mountain peak was briefly visible. And that's when the girl saw the faint outline of rooftops and even a steeple or tower of some kind.

Her parents had never spoken of other villages, and when she asked them about it, pointed at it, they claimed not to see it. No one else saw the village. Her little sister said she did see it, but this was the same sister who followed her in everything she said—green was also her favorite color, she also liked to wear her hair in three ponytails, and, like the girl, she enjoyed burying dead animals and digging them up again.

During her childhood and adolescence, the girl never stopped looking at the distant mountain, hoping to see the village again. Every time she thought of the village, a feeling opened up in her stomach that then saturated her entire body. If she had been asked to put it into words, she would say it was a rush, a lifting off the ground, almost. It was a wave of awareness, clear and sharp, of so much more than this: more than this village, more than these familiar streets, and more than these people and their endless town hall meetings.

It was a wave that swept her far away from the entire structure that was village life, into something far more wild and yet also peaceful. If she had been asked to put the feeling the other village gave her into one word, she would probably say it was "longing." It was the closest she would ever get to describing it, but no one asked her to put it into words, because they did not believe in the village and in new feelings that were never articulated before, and she talked about the village only with her sister, who never asked any questions at all.

At night, when the girl lay in bed, she searched her mind for the image of the village, and she let the feeling surge through her body, and she reveled in knowing that it was there.

"There is no village," her father said sometimes when he saw her faraway eyes as she led the sheep into the fields in the morning. And he added, "If there was another village, it is too far away."

Only two more times she saw actual evidence of this village: once she saw a light reflected up there, a repeated quick flashing, and another time she heard goat bells clanging in the distance.

After her mother's unexpected death from the coughing disease, the girl had a harder time reaching the feeling at night. When she looked at the distant mountain during the day, her stomach did not leap, and the voices of her fellow villagers remained loud and clear in her ears.

When spring came, the girl set out to climb the mountain, to get closer to the village. She told no one and quietly made her preparations. She braided her hair in the lasting way, she ate a lot so she had some extra weight to use up, she made a backpack with a knife and a water container. Then she waited for a day when the seagulls flew low, and when such a day came, she set out to "paradise village," as she called it in her mind.

The journey was less challenging than she expected. In fact, it was easy. For three days and nights she walked and slept alongside the waterfall that had carved a path through the mountains. After three days she discovered a barely noticeable trail of wooden beams leading into the forest that someone seemed to have made a long time ago. On the fifth night of her journey she reached the top of the mountain. And there it was: the other village. It was surrounded by a circular wall made from pale yellow stone, and a symbol of a bird was carved into the arch above the only gate.

The girl stood there gazing at it for a long time. Her stomach leaped in the familiar way, and the feeling that she might call "longing" saturated her body again, from her ears to the tips of her toes. In this calm but elated state, she made a little shelter in the woods just outside the village. From this spot she could see the lights going on behind the village walls when the evening came, a warm orange glow rising up into the twilight. She saw what it was that had reflected the light that one day: a bird sculpture that was mounted on top of a tower turned with the wind. It must have caught the sun at just the right angle.

She spent a clear night under the stars outside the village, going in and out of sleep. When the village gate opened in the morning with a loud creaking, she hid behind a big rock. A man came out with a herd of goats. Through the open gate, the girl caught glimpses of a market. People were walking in a village square carrying straw baskets, stopping to talk to each other, just like in her village back home. The difference was that their coats were long and square and looked like they were made of black goat wool, while in her village people wore their coats short, and they were made of light sheep wool.

At this moment, the girl wished to go home. She did not want to go inside the other village or announce herself. Instead, she made the trek back to her own village and went to bed without telling anyone what she had seen.

She did not go back to the other village for a long time. But every time she looked in the distance, the feeling surged in her stomach again.

Once every few years, when it was spring and the weather was calm, the girl made the trek up again and spent another night watching the other village. She did not try to see more than the previous time; she just observed the walls and the roofs and caught that short glimpse of the village square when the gate opened for the herder.

As the girl became a woman, she found her role in her own village as head of the library, where she guarded and maintained every book the villagers had ever written. Reading books somehow felt a little bit similar to going to the other village, even though she had no idea why and how that was so. When she was older, the woman wrote a short book herself, about the paradise village and how thinking of it could make you feel something new, but only the children in her village were interested in the book.

During the winter, when everything was quiet and parents had time to listen to their children, the adults of the town became uneasy by their talk of a "new feeling" and a "new village." They sent the mayor to the library to solve it. The mayor took off his coat and hat, politely looked at a few books with simulated interest, and then asked her not to confuse the children anymore with tales of villages that weren't actually there and feelings that weren't actually in existence. And if there was another village, he said, lowering his voice, there would be none of this nonsense of not going inside.

"First, I would send someone to count how many people there are in this village, to see if we are outnumbered. Then

I, as mayor, would go there personally and trade sardine oil against their goats."

The mayor explained how it would be his obligation to tell this other village about customs and laws and the right way of doing things, and how he would make sure they knew they needed to bathe their babies twice on their first full moon. It would be important to know how their women smelled, he added, if they smelled differently from ours.

The woman cast her eyes down. She quietly said that the book was not about this, that it was just some idea of reaching something very old and very deep inside of us, not something new outside of us. And that probably she had been mistaken, that this feeling did not exist. For sure there was no other village after all. It had been a dream, a delusion, caused by sitting in the library for so long.

The mayor shook his head at her carelessness, but since it was exactly in line with what he had thought of her all along, he did not think much more about it, and he put on his coat to do something more urgent, like inspecting the fortification of the village wall.

Then spring came, and fresh sardines came to the coast, and everyone forgot about other villages and other feelings. The woman never mentioned them again. She simply continued to make her trek once every few years. As she got older the climbing was harder, but she had uncovered most of the old path, and she had made a rope banister along the steep parts that helped her climb.

On one of her journeys, something unexpected happened. She was followed. The woman discovered her secret follower only when she heard someone yelp out in pain behind her. It was her younger sister, who now was also in her sixties. She had slipped on a stone and got her foot stuck between two big rocks. The woman helped her out of there, and they made the rest of the journey together. Quietly they installed themselves in her shelter in the woods just outside the other village, sharing the small space as they watched a kite rise up behind the village walls.

They watched in silence as the lights turned on in the village, an orange hue against the hard blue clouds, and they watched in silence when the goat herder came out of the gate the next morning.

As they packed up their things in the morning light to return to their own village, her sister looked at the woman.

"You don't go in," her sister said.

"I don't go in," the woman said.

The Angel and the Little Witch

A STONE HOUSE STOOD just outside the village gate, ten steps from the bridge over the river that coiled like a snake around the village. In that house lived the little witch. This story is about her and the three times an angel came to her and told her to love herself.

The first time this happened, the little witch was in bed. It was long after midnight, but she was still awake; she had made potions all night for villagers who were suffering from the eczema that returned each year around this time. She was looking up at the ceiling from her bed, thinking of one specific villager, a watch repairman named Pierre. He had called her "that crazy witch" in the town meeting that day. Her elderly father had been at the meeting, and he had passed this news on to her when she visited him to bring him his daily dinner. She could see on his face it had caused him shame. "Why did you not say I was your daughter?" she wanted to ask, but her father had already moved on to another topic. He was telling a story he loved to tell, about a time when he was a young boy and he found a yellow ball his brothers had lost.

"For hours they looked for the ball," her father told her. "They looked behind every tree and in every ditch, until I had the sudden inclination to look up. And sure enough, there it was, the yellow ball, stuck between the branch and the trunk of a tree!" This story pleased her father very much, and she saw why he told it right after telling her about the watchmaker Pierre who caused him shame. The little witch had heard the yellow ball story many times before, and she had commented many times before that it takes a special man to look where no one thought to look, to turn his chin up toward the sky, when everyone is gazing at the ground.

She grimaced in bed as she thought of how she had indulged her father. But it was good that she indulged him, she reminded herself. Why would she keep an old man from having these little pleasures? When she would be old, when she would be *older*, she would also be forgetful. And she would hope that people would extend the same kind of forgiveness to her. A vague sadness drifted through her half-sleeping body, a sadness she often felt when she realized she would never be cared for the way she cared for others.

At that moment, the angel came to her for the first time, and he said, "You have to love yourself."

The angel disappeared, and the little witch was left alone in her bed. She got up and looked in the mirror and tried to love herself. She looked at the icy eyes, the thin hands, the round bones on her wrists, the freckles on her arms, and the soft belly, and all she felt was ambivalence. What did the feeling of love have to do with it? Does dog love dog? Her body was a fact, as was the dark, starry sky above the house and the pond in the garden and the cold stone tiles under her feet.

She then tried to love not her body but her person. She contemplated her achievements, her habits, her preoccupations. She pictured herself from a bird's-eye view: how she walked down to the market each day, nodding politely at everyone; how she brought her father soft dinners because he could not chew anymore; how she often stopped by to say hello to Madame Schwartz, who was losing it; and how she made the remedies late at night for everyone who needed it, even when they spoke badly of her. It was something, sure, but was it enough to love? She had wasted most of her life being distracted by something or another. She always ran out of money in summer, when no one got sick, and had to ask for an extension on the rent. The dinners she made for her father were often quick and lazy, leek soup and mashed potatoes. She neglected her body, she never had followed through on her plan to make a potion against eczema that would last longer than one season, and, on top of that, she was irritable, messy, shy, and judgmental.

A person she could imagine herself loving would have to be a much better version of her. Someone who would not shuffle so close to the walls, who would keep her hair neat and take up space in a dignified manner. Someone who wouldn't just nod at others but converse thoughtfully and make charming observations. Someone who would not scamper away from eye contact. This person she imagined loving would stand tall and patient. She would perhaps have a market stall with long-lasting remedies in the middle of the village square. Yes, that is what it would have to be, a beautiful stall, instead of how it was now, where people came to her house at all hours, and she let them pay whatever they felt like because she could not bear the idea of haggling and the eye contact that went with it.

The next day the little witch carefully combed her hair, soaked her skin in honey, and wrapped up her remedies in paper with neatly tied strings. She put the remedies on display in the market, on her garden table that she dragged all the way over the bridge and through the village gate. The mineral stone seller instantly came over to complain that she obscured the view to his stall, and then the butcher came to say her potions reeked and he did not want her in front of his shop. She tried to stand tall and patient as she listened to them. And though she felt shy, she held their gaze, even as she saw the fear in their eyes and could feel it seeping into her body too.

Eventually she agreed to move to the steps of the library, with her merchandise table in front of her. She tried to reply thoughtfully to each person who inquired about the treatments, but she soon grew irritated with their long-winded complaints about their petty ailments, and she also got tired of sitting up tall because carrying the table had hurt her back. At noon the little witch wrapped up what remained of the remedies, and she muttered some inaudible excuse to whoever was standing in front of her at that moment. Then she dragged her table away.

When she got home she felt so tired, so exhausted, from all the little stories that the people in the village had told her, not only with the things they said but also through the way they moved their eyebrows, the trembling of their hands, the choice of one word over another, the way they positioned their feet. The softer sound of the baker's voice told the little witch he was once again feeling the back of his wife's hand against his cheek in the evenings, and the way the butcher gave her that little smile told her he disliked her still. She knew this little smile from when he was annoyed with her for ordering one small steak from the premium cut of beef—he did not like to slice a fine piece of meat for just one steak. She could see the fear beneath that little smile—the fear of losing everything—and she knew this fear came from the butcher's father, whose unnerved darting eye movements had not escaped her as a little girl. She also knew it was the butcher's father's father who had caused it all, because she had heard stories of how he had caused the family much uncertainty and shame with his reckless gambling.

The little witch knew too much, and it was exhausting. Even the joyful things depleted her sometimes, the way the rain touched her skin made her so full of emotion, it just picked her up and carried her too far away from that thing called "daily life," too far away from the alertness needed to be a remedy-seller, a rent-payer, a coin-counter, a good-woman.

"How am I supposed to love this little witch?" she thought when she looked in the mirror. Her hair was a tangled mess yet again. She was too late to make her father a proper supper, so it would be soup for him, like it or not. And she could not muster the energy to store away the scraps of paper and string scattered around the floor, remnants from her eager wrapping that morning.

"One cannot generate the feeling of love out of nothing," she thought, "like one cannot light a fire on a cold stone floor without any firewood. I cannot lie to myself about who I am, and I cannot delude myself into thinking highly of my achievements."

A few days later the angel came to her a second time. She had gathered wood for the fire, and she was getting into bed feeling tired, smelling faintly of wood, and thinking of the many-legged bug she had seen crawling in the cellar. The experience with the angel was the same as before, only this time the little witch yelled out, "How?" when the angel suggested she love herself. Again he disappeared. She slept very little that night, lying awake for a long time thinking of how she had already tried to love herself and how it did not work, and why there were only such narrow and stupid road maps made for developing the spirit, why they had to be full of riddles and platitudes, and why it was always male angels who appeared to her.

The next day at the market, the little witch rushed through her shopping. She requested a second-rate piece of meat from the butcher so he would not make the face that wounded her, and she muttered at people who started a conversation. All she wanted was to go home quickly and sleep some more. "Is that not loving myself?" she thought. "Giving in to what I need is surely a form of love." But already she knew that was not it, she already knew she would feel bad in the evening when she ate the second-rate meat. As she crossed the river, kids from town emerged to throw rocks at her and yell "witch." They had done it before; it was just pebbles, and usually she hid behind her basket and rushed on, knowing that people fear only what they don't understand. This time, though, she could not do it.

She stopped, and for a brief moment the little witch felt a clarity inside her. It was like a little orange light, glowing in the depths of her stomach. It felt very good. She stayed like that for a while, just feeling the orange light inside of her.

When a stone hit her thigh and a sharp pain shot through her body, the little witch found herself suddenly turning around and walking up to the boys. In a voice that seemed to come from far beyond herself she bellowed, "Stop it! What are you doing, throwing rocks at me? If your mother gets eczema I won't treat her, and it will be your fault, because you are horrid little creatures! Go away, go away now, before I hurt you!" The boys scurried away.

The little witch wanted to turn back to the little orange light that had lit up inside of her, but it was gone. Instead, only her heart thumped fast in her chest. But she knew that this thing that she felt, that moment of orange light, that was it—that was what the angel had talked about.

"Maybe," she thought, "loving yourself has to do with anger." For so many years she had accepted everyone calling her a witch—even the teller of this story calls her a witch like it is all normal and acceptable—but she was not taking it anymore. She was Helen, and she was not a witch, and she was not to be thrown rocks at. And why should she take the second-rate cut from the butcher? He should just hurry up and help her! Immediately she turned back to the village and demanded her premium steak from the butcher, cutting in front of the line and reminding him in a loud voice how she had cured his wife from the blistering illness. A piece of first-rate steak was produced swiftly with compliments, and a couple of fresh eggs wrapped in fabric were given to her as well.

She did not thank him or smile. She went to her father to make him an omelet. The eggs reminded him of the story of how he found the yellow ball everyone was looking for, stuck between the branch and the trunk of a tree overhead. As her father marveled at his ability to think of something that no one thought of, the little witch felt her throat tighten.

"Do you realize you tell me this story every time I see you?" she asked her father. "Do you realize how you seek to be praised every time?"

Her father looked up from his omelet, too stunned to deny it.

The little witch continued, her voice firm and sharp: "They did not think to look up, but surprise! You did! Some people spend their entire lives staring down at the ground, but not you! You looked up! What a genius you are, Father, what an underestimated person. If everyone would just listen to you, then things would be much better."

Her father muttered something about the moral of the story, about what else might be there but we don't see it, but he stopped when he saw her face, and he thanked her for bringing him dinner every night so kindly.

The next days the little witch, I mean Helen, did the same at every store and market stall, telling everyone the truth and shutting down their defensive responses. She confronted her cousin who took her garden plot and never paid for it, and she went to the watchmaker Pierre who had said she was a crazy witch to ask him to say it to her face. She asserted herself with each and every person, and she finally got her due after all these years. People paid for the remedies she gave them; they knocked on her door before entering; they did not cut in line in front of her anymore. Everyone who had ever wronged her avoided her, which is to say everyone, because everyone wrongs everyone all the time.

In the evenings, Helen sat alone in her little house, her sturdy heart pounding, with a tender piece of steak in front of her. It was a lonely time, as would be expected, but also a great relief. She could breathe more easily and speak more clearly. In fact, she was certain she could even see farther when she went out on the plains. But not once did she feel the orange light in her lower belly. She tried to summon it, but it was like holding a match to a bare stone floor. It wouldn't burn.

The third time the angel came to her was when she was lying in bed in the late afternoon, staring angrily at the ceiling. "Go away," she said with an annoyance that was sounding a little rehearsed by now. "I already know what you are going to say. Why can't you be clearer? Why must you always speak in riddles and symbols and half stories? I don't even believe in you! You look exactly like the drawing in my third grade history book. Go away! Go away!"

She shut her eyes tight in protest and covered her ears. When she opened them again the angel had gone away. She never heard him say "You must love yourself," though she was right—that was precisely what he had said to her. She sat up in bed ruminating until the morning came. Despite her reluctance to believe in the angel's message, she kept turning the words over and over again in her head. "Love yourself, love yourself," she thought. "What even is it? Appreciate? Tolerate? Celebrate? Accept? Pity? Honor? Care for?"

All those things she could do toward others, but when she tried to turn the arrows of those feelings onto herself, they bent and slipped right past her. She wasn't sure if she ever had any feelings toward herself in that way. How could she feel something about herself as she was inside herself?

In her nightgown the little witch walked out into her garden, finding her way through the dark early morning by feeling the edges of the path with her feet. She sat down by the pond. The mud seeped between her toes, and the stars were vague dots above her. For a long time she sat there and thought about how annoying angels were, how annoying the whole religion thing was and God too, how annoying the people in town were, how annoying life . . . life . . . what the hell was it even? Why was she, some little creature, sitting by a thing called a "pond" in a thing called the "night"? What was the point of it? She wondered all these things, though she knew there was no point to any of it, and that was the whole point.

When her head got tired she pulled her feet from the water. The sun was rising, and she saw the light reflecting on the greenish pond. Shimmering water slid across a flat gray stone, then retreated again.

At that moment, the little orange light lit up inside the little witch again.

This time, she was very cautious not to disturb it. Very carefully, she brought herself and the light back into the house, as if she were carrying a candle that she was shielding against the wind, and she sat down at her kitchen table very, very gently. The orange light stayed with her and filled her with a pleasant sensation. Only when the thought "I got it" occurred to her, the light went out again. The little witch did not try to get it back. She went to sleep, somehow knowing that the light would come back the next day, and it did. She spent the next weeks befriending the light like she had once befriended a baby deer in the forest: waiting for it in familiar places, sitting down next to it, watching it, letting it come closer to her.

While getting steak at the butcher, while foraging for mushrooms in the forest, while treating an infected ear, the little witch kept a part of her attention on the orange light all the time. She moved only very little in her mind and in conversation. After a while, she was able to keep the light going for several days in a row, while going about her daily life, dividing her attention between her light and the world around her.

Often when she was treating people, the light flared up a little higher. She had become softer and more cheerful. Whether she let people cut in line in front of her at the bakery or she didn't, whether she got a face from the butcher when she asked for the premium cut or not, whether her father was ashamed of her—not of it mattered so much anymore. She loved herself, as the angel had put it, and she remembered she had always done so when she was young.

Actually, she would say that what she was doing was not loving herself, which sounded like something that you do to yourself from the outside. She would not call it "doing" at all. It was just an orange light inside herself that she kept an eye on, that she didn't need to do anything for. It was just there, like some miraculous fire emerging from a stone floor.

The little witch did not get her own market stall in the end; she did not like dragging the table. People came to her house at all hours still, but they knocked, and when she was tired of them she sent them away. In summer she was still short of money, and when it rained she still let it distract her from her work and she wandered into the fields to enjoy how it touched her skin. One time she forgot she was making soup in a moment like that and the house nearly burned down, so she hadn't learned much. There were not many big changes in her life at all, except that she felt like when she was a child again, sitting happily in the lap of the universe.

And when the angel came back to tell her, "I told you so," she could only laugh at him, and he laughed at her.

Guided

Thumbs

"THE BLUE LINE at the base of your thumb will fade over time, but it will never completely go away," the doctor in charge of aftercare in the Guided Facility said as she took the bandages off my right hand. "As you probably know."

My newborn thumb slowly appeared as the layers of white gauze were being unwrapped. It looked just like my original thumb, except exceptionally pink and the nail still was yet to grow in. I knew the thumb would be printed from my personal cells and based on a scan of my left one, but I had been worried it would feel alien. It did not. It felt mine.

"It's nice to be symmetrical again," I told the doctor.

"A Guided probe has been implanted in your right thumb, in place of the proximal phalanx," she said. "The program will be activated in an hour on a twenty percent setting to ease you into it. We will work up to one hundred percent over the next forty-eight hours, while monitoring your neural responses and your pituitary gland. This room is your monitoring field, so don't leave it." She laughed. "Unless you want to, of course."

I nodded. The First Law of Free Will: No coercion. The first and only law of Guided society.

"Visitors will be unaffected by the field, if you are expecting any," the doctor continued.

"I am expecting a visitor," I said. "Well, 'hoping' might be a better word . . . if she will ever forgive me."

"'Forgiveness' is an UnGuided word." The doctor smiled.

I tried to smile back.

"If you are feeling scared to see your loved ones, or anxious to go back on Guided, then just remind yourself that you don't have to do anything with those scared feelings," she said. "The fear will disappear on its own. All the pain will fade."

I assured the doctor that even though she had read my body language well—I *was* scared to go back on Guided—I was not having doubts. If I had learned anything during my time with the UnGuided, it was that feelings of fear often lack a rational source. Yes, I was anxious, but rationally the choice to go back to Guided living was the right one. It was going to be wonderful to ditch all these dreadful feelings. Especially now that I was about to get my period, which made me even more prone to emotional instability.

"You can do some coloring fields if you want to relax," the doctor said as she gave me a coloring tablet. "Do you like math? There's a beautiful 4D one with numbered Vedic squares. Or you can watch our history program. The command code of the perception field is AGF, from Amsterdam Guided Facility."

The doctor disappeared into the hallway of the Guided Facility, leaving behind a scent of disinfectant. I looked at my left original thumb. Then I looked at my pink artificial thumb. It was throbbing where the Guided probe was implanted. It was sitting invisible under my skin again, like a little factory. My stomach felt like I was falling; a wave of anxiety rolled up through my body. I closed my eyes, trying to remember the lines from the UnGuided Handbook that we recited when we felt panic. Forty-eight hours from now I would not need them anymore, so I allowed myself to recite them once more until they calmed me down. "There are many ways," I whispered. "Disruption is the natural state. Change is in the fabric of a day."

Jane

FROM THE WINDOW by my bed on the thirteenth floor of the Amsterdam Guided Facility, I could see most of southern Amsterdam. The flamingos that settled in Amsterdam in the late 2000s walked with slow, long paces through the shallow end of the Vondelpark lake. Kids played on the grass, their parents running after them. All of them were *leaving their belongings unattended* on their picnic blankets. That was part of a familiar phrase from the early twenty-first century, which I had just learned from watching the Guided history program. If people in those days left their belongings unattended in public, the voice-over of the Guided history program had explained, someone else would likely come by and snatch their belongings and run off with them. So in those days, recorded announcements often reminded people: "Do not leave belongings unattended." There was another reason not to do such a thing: unattended belongings could also be mistaken for improvised explosive devices, left behind by violent terrorists.

My comrades—my former comrades, I have to say!—from the UnGuided community had warned me that I would be shown these "Guided propaganda shows" in the facility. To me the history program did not seem like propaganda but exactly what it claimed to be: an unbiased history of how global society embraced artificial group intelligence. There was no such thing as propaganda in the Guided society.

What would they (*we*, I needed to remember to start saying *we*) need propaganda for? Peace, safety, equality, transparency, health, and happiness for all didn't need a sales talk. It was 2152, and everyone was finally happy.

"AGF, resume *History of Guided* program," I said, and the perception field in my room switched on.

"In the early 2000s people's lives were not in tune with each other," the narrator said over the video fields of dozens of people pushing one another into a packed underground train. "In constant conflict with those around them and with themselves, the lives of these people were full of failure, humiliation, stress, and disappointment. People's awareness of the mutations inside themselves and others were limited, they could use only their own senses and some crude and expensive external technologies. Therapies and philosophies were used by individuals to try to gain more control over psychological and physical challenges, which were often still treated as two separate elements. With the help of early external so-called smart devices, crude elements of the functioning of the body could be mapped. Counting the footsteps taken during the day, for instance, or the hours of sleep. People hoped this would help them have more control over their own behavior, and they allowed the devices to give them behavioral suggestions such as 'breathe deeply.'"

The program showed an array of clunky wrist devices from the Amsterdam UnGuided Museum collection. I knew what they looked like; my great-grandfather used to have one of those devices. It was called a Fitbit. My grandmother held on to it, and with her permission, I took it to school once, to accompany my presentation on the topic of group harmony.

"It counted your steps," I remember I said in a dramatic tone to my classmates as I held up the device, "but it also was the first step to world peace." I remembered how the whole classroom marveled at the minimal services you got in return for hanging such a huge apparatus from your arm.

"Health apps and devices became increasingly popular," the history program narrator continued. "And in 2028 a simple update was launched that would turn out to be world changing. UnitGuide. By using this app, people could link their health data with someone else they wanted to form a unit with. They could read the other's heart rate, sleep quality, and breathing tempo, but the app also analyzed the influence they had on each other. The behavioral suggestions the app offered benefited the optimal functioning of the unit, not the individual. Examples of these still very basic suggestions were 'listen, don't speak' and 'initiate long hug.' The problem with these suggestions was the amount of self-control that was required of people to follow them. A wife in the early twenty-first century might not be able to persuade herself to give her husband a 'long hug' in the middle of an argument, even though it would prevent escalation. It took two decades until a solution for this was found. An on-site clinic at the UnitGuide campus started offering an electrochemical probe to employees, which stimulated the release of certain hormones in accordance with the app's behavioral suggestions. The app and probe combination was called iGuided. It was the earliest version of what we now simply know as Guided."

At that moment, the history program paused. Someone was pressing the buzzer to my hospital room.

"Jane?" I called, sitting up straight in the hospital bed. "AGF, open door."

From the hallway the familiar gray carry-on bag first emerged, that hideous thing Jane took everywhere, followed by my girlfriend, or maybe ex-girlfriend, something I was going to find out soon enough.

"Jane, I want to explain," I started, but she immediately raised her hand to stop me talking.

"I don't need to know why you did it, because I do not believe you have sufficient insight into your motivations," Jane said, sitting down on the chair next to my bed. "I am willing to take you back if you get through the Disruption Test successfully." She paused for a moment and looked out the window. White clouds were moving slowly under the blue sky. "Additionally, you should know I threw all your possessions away after twelve months, everything except your university diploma and your jewelry, which I gave to your parents. I am also dating someone, but I have informed them I am still attached to you."

I was surprised by her little speech. She was already considering taking me back. I abandoned her, the house, and the dog for fourteen months, and this was her first response.

"It won't happen again," I said. "Never." I noticed my voice was softer and had less intonation. The switching on of the Guided probe in my right thumb must have taken place. An already noticeable flattening of my feelings. A pleasant sense of calm trickling through my body. The tone and register of my voice calibrating to hers, as I noticed my upper body moving slightly away. Our Guides were communicating. Jane wanted physical distance, and I couldn't blame her.

"Daisy is fine, by the way," she said, zipping open the carry-on bag and taking out boxes with falafel and hummus. "She did hurt her paw somehow when you left her in the forest—must have gotten stuck on something as she was making her way home. It took three months to heal."

"I am sorry," I said. "If you knew how much I regret leaving her behind like that . . . I kept lying awake with guilt, loathing myself, thinking, 'How could I?' Our dog of eight years . . . I am so sorry."

"As I said, it has healed," Jane said.

For a moment it was quiet. Then, quite suddenly, I realized I had used all kinds of UnGuided words: "regret" and "guilt" and "loathing." How was J supposed to react to that? Fear and insecurity rose up inside of me. I wanted to ask Jane to reassure me, like we did in the UnGuided community, embracing each other and reassuring ourselves with soft words and caresses. But that would only make me seem more alien.

"How much are you on right now?" she asked, nodding at my thumb.

"Twenty percent," I said. "They start it there, at twenty percent." My voice was shaky, anxiety breaking through the low Guided dose. "I want you to know I am not an Undercover," I told Jane.

"That would be your Free Will," Jane said, shrugging. "What are you watching?"

She nodded at the frozen perception field hanging over the foot end of my bed.

"AGF, continue program," I said, glad to have something to focus on other than Jane's resentful shrugs—or what I perceived as resentful, because being resentful was an Un-Guided state.

Together we watched how iGuided evolved from individual to societal use. An old 2D television advertisement showed a muscled man who said in an animated voice, "Did you know that people who are low on dopamine make irrational decisions? It's a natural response. The body tries to find satisfaction by doing absurd things that induce dopamine hits, like eating doughnuts, flirting with a 'work wife,' or getting addicted to online gambling or porn. Things that make you feel bad! Things *you* don't want to do! By using iGuided, you will be able to maintain diets, get through job interviews and first dates without nerves, and your marital arguments will never spiral out of control again. This thing can save your life!"

Quietly J and I watched footage of a man and woman in the gender roles of that era; he was coming home from work with a briefcase, she was preparing food in the kitchen. Before he sticks a key in the door's traditional keyhole, the man checks his wife's status on his wrist device. "Zara: Heart rate high. Breathing fast." The man smiles. He turns around and comes back with takeaway food and a bottle of wine. The woman embraces him. A burned meal is visible on the stove, which is what they called those toxic gas-fire contraptions they burned inside their own homes back then.

I looked sideways at Jane, who was smiling at the perception field. She was holding her little box of homemade hummus on her lap, absentmindedly stroking it as if it were Daisy. Was she thinking about the same things as I was? How nice it would be to come home to our cottage again; to cook together, have tea together, work side by side at the desk; to walk Daisy together; to have friends over; to have everything fall back into place.

"I've missed you," I said, putting my hand on hers.

"I missed you too," she said, taking her hand away. "But our connection will be better when you are fully Guided again."

She got up and placed the boxes of food in the small fridge by my bed. I realized it was unpleasant for her to be around me. The lack of Guidance that kept me from moving harmoniously with her. All the feelings that were showing on my face. For her, it was like sitting next to an insane person. I knew that, because that's how I felt during my first days in the UnGuided community.

Jane bent over the bed and kissed me. She smelled delicious like always, like soap and seawater. "See you later," she said.

Wrinkles

As I sat on my bed eating spoonfuls of hummus, I thought about J's reaction to me. I remembered one day, when we were out shopping and came across an UnGuided art performance, she turned to me and said, "Poor people . . . Did you see the wrinkles on that woman's forehead? It must be true that they sleep very poorly. But I always wonder why they have to smell so bad. Surely having more feelings doesn't prevent you from bathing."

I got out of my hospital bed and looked in the mirror above the sink. Thirty-five years old. The braids I wore in the UnGuided community were cut off by the hospital hairdresser at my request. The haircut he subsequently gave me looked very similar to my old pixie cut. But consternation remained on my face, etched like a Roman numeral *II* between my eyebrows. I also had laugh lines around my eyes and creases around the edges of my mouth. Needless to say, Jane hadn't acquired any new wrinkles while I was gone.

Behind me the voice-over of the history program continued: "Around 2060 the use of the app and probe combination, now simply named Guided, started to become mainstream. Job ads often featured the sentence: 'Guided folks encouraged to apply.' Offices using the GuidedTeam sync option reported better results, higher productivity, less sick leave, and, to their own surprise, a stronger ethical foundation. Couples advised other couples to get Guided as a unit when the marriage was under strain from a newborn or a lost job. 'We'll switch it off and fight the big fights when times are better,' they often said. But a logical discovery was that those fights did not need to be fought. More in sync and never in a chemically deprived state, the needs of the unit were met and the problematic reactions that came out under duress—neediness, anger, fear, and resentment—were avoided. Guided holiday dinners became something of a cultural phenomena. In the past, annual family dinners, such as those during Eid or Christmas celebrations, were a source of emotional duress for many. But when the family members were using Guided, they did not react to one another from a state of panic. They could have their arguments without reenacting family patterns of overruling others or playing the victim. When one family member got overheated, the UnitFit feature made sure the others became calm. Soon it became less necessary to even have the argument. In the United States, where Guided was first widely used, political tensions dissipated. A little Guidance helped humanity make quick progress. Greed was lessened by the increase of happiness; income inequality decreased for the first time in centuries. Political leaders with moderate views got more votes. The hate and fear of people of a different sexuality, gender, color, or culture seemed ridiculous suddenly. Divorce rates dropped, children had more stable homes, and the obesity crisis of the past century was tamed through the impulse control Guided provided."

"I was afraid this thing would turn me into a robot," a man with a beard said to his phone camera in that typical twenty-first-century self-obsessed manner. "Instead, I finally feel like myself. And you hardly see it!"

That final comment, I had to admit from my privileged twenty-second-century standpoint, was not quite true. To me, the two-centimeter rectangular implant under the skin of that guy's upper arm looked pretty creepy in comparison to our invisible plasma-coated biotech probe. But clunky as it was, the implant clearly worked. Of course it worked. Our time was proof of that. So much had changed since then. No more war. No more greed. No more stealing. No more inequality. No more homelessness. A utopian socialist-anarchist-capitalist hybrid system. I thought of the parents in the park. Much more significant than leaving their belongings unattended was the fact that in their world (in *our* world, I have to start saying again!) parents could leave their children unattended. To be able to live without the fear of child abductions, child abuse, child murder, who would ever choose against that?

As if the history program could read my thoughts, the voice-over said, "The cause of the final push toward mass Guidance was simple: our children. After the Third Lockdown happened in 2062—an antibiotic-resistant strain of MRSA bacteria that badly affected children—scientists pointed out the possibility of utilizing Guided. Until that day, the system was used mostly for small groups: the family, the couple, the team, the company. Guiding the entire society toward a better collaboration was a new step. The data gathered would help identify infected persons and guide the masses away from areas with higher rates of infection risk. The unit feature could make lockdown safer and more pleasant."

"Yes, it is scary to put our information and daily decisions into the hands of others, even if they are trusted scientists," prime ministers and presidents from all over the world said in a joint statement that interrupted all holo-calls, video games, and Real-Streams. "But if we claim to want to live in a society, we need to have a level of trust with others. We also allow our cars to drive us at an agreed-upon speed and block us from going faster, because we don't want to act like we are the only ones on the road; we take the medications the doctors suggest because they know more; we put on clothes, because we agreed on that with each other; we pay taxes so everyone can go to schools and hospitals. We would like to think that this ability to care for others, next door and familiar or many miles away and unknown, is what makes us human. Let's do it for the children."

"This speech resulted in mass protests and riots around the world. In Amsterdam it culminated in the famous burning of the palace on Dam Square. Since the incubation time of this bacterial infection was fourteen days, on the fifteenth day the majority of the protesters fell ill. This day became known as Red Monday—a reference to the skin inflammation caused by the bacteria. Many of the protesters passed the bacteria on to children in their environment. And while the adults survived, the children died of sepsis. The backlash from families caused many of the opponents to join the Guided program after all. Those who remained opposed became unwelcome in their own communities. The anti-Guided people were assigned territories, where they formed alternative societies that were, more or less, based on the way things were in the years before Guided. The members of the anti-Guided group were from many different backgrounds but were united by a shared delusion that Guided was unnatural. This fractured group became known as the 'UnGuided.'"

Delusion. I asked the perception field for a definition of "delusion": "Having a false fixed belief that remains unchanged in the face of conflicting evidence."

That was correct: every single person I met in the UnGuided community had a delusion. The delusion was that there could be something better than Guided. That there were many ways, not just one. The delusion was that we would find a way, or several ways, to have peace and happiness without the Guided system.

"Patience and empathy do not have to be manufactured," Ali used to tell me. "We can all be happy, if we do not give up on finding ways."

I thought of her brother's face when he found her body. A painful sadness made its way up my spine. I checked my Guided levels. The probe was now set at 40 percent.

Bliss

As the afternoon turned into evening, I tried to do some coloring, but I could not concentrate. I just sat on the bed and tried to feel the changes in my body. The curtain of my hospital room moved in the wind, the sun playing with patterns on the ceiling. I noticed I felt nothing, just a careless, pleasant nothing. I remembered a time, not too long ago, when that delicate curtain dance would give me a feeling of awe, a sense of entwining with the light, a delicious twisting and falling. The little probe in my thumb prevented that feeling from ever recurring in my body again.

This was the only thing truly missing in Guided society. What I think is called "bliss."

No matter how much Guided society had tried to construct it, this feeling of bliss was absent in the Guided world. They—we! I have to say we!—experience euphoria, ecstasy, climax. But not bliss. Bliss was a longer, calmer state and seemed to be dependent on some kind of contrast or "discord," as they used to call it in music. The word "bliss" wasn't commonly used anymore, and when someone did say it, it sounded as ancient as "cassette recorder," "rapist," or "horse carriage."

The voice-over of the history program interrupted my thoughts. "The day our society was declared free of MRSA-62, a bonus serotonin release was given to the people as a treat. This triggered a global party, and the resulting baby boom nine months later proved that the probe did not diminish sexual appetite. The anger and strife people of the previous century seemed to believe was needed for lust and passion had gone, but sex and pleasure survived. A new generation grew up who never knew what it was like not to be Guided, or at least live in a world where others weren't Guided."

Of course, I was one of that generation.

"Nature is flawed," I remembered little ten-year-old me declaring during that school presentation. "As I am speaking, some baby hippo is watching its starving mother being slowly eaten alive by crocodiles in the Nile, a mother wolf is mating with her own son because in season these urges take over. That is fine for the animals, but as humanity we had the luck to be more evolved than that and take some of it into our own hands. If we think it was natural to start using a hammer, then what is unnatural about this tool? Perhaps one day we could even guide the animals toward a new civilization too."

My presentation had been part of the school Herd Harmony program, which encouraged a critical approach. Many teenagers, including some of my classmates from the Amsterdam Ignatius College, went through a phase where they rebelled against the app. Some of them wanted it turned down, which was not that easy because making it hack-proof also meant it was nearly impossible to alter it. The debate program was started as a way to show the teens that in a free society, their rebellious ideas and thoughts were encouraged, not suppressed.

Though one could say that being allowed to express ideas does not exactly mean freedom. If you can't act on them, what is the point in expressing them? The only option to get out of the Guided system was—and is—to amputate the right thumb that had the Guided implant, which most kids were too smart or too Guided to do. The few kids who went through with it reported to the hospital within days, absolutely terrified by their own inner life. "Paralyzing fear and confusion, irrational irritability, and total lack of mental clarity," is how Sal, my old school friend, described UnGuided life when I saw him at university. He was wearing a ring around his right thumb, covering the scar. He now worked as a biochemist at the Guided Clinic. People who had become UnGuided as youngsters often became the most fervent promotors of the Guided state.

"All the decisions made by the Guided system are direct translations of the group's desires. Everything we do at Guided Facilities is fully transparent and in line with the First Law," the voice-over continued as drone footage of the Guided Facility in Amsterdam was shown. I squeezed my eyes to try to make out the floor I was on. "The fears people had in the twenty-first century—governments using the systems to make their people docile, evil corporations taking advantage, a select few playing the others like puppets—did not happen, simply because Guided people are beyond infantile urges like greed, power hunger, and self-aggrandizement. Guided has little influence on people's ability to think critically and analyze. In fact, our capability for being self-critical and to change increased, as evidenced by the quick reversal of the ecological crisis of the twentieth and twenty-first century. The only undeniable downside of Guided is that we, as humanity, have lost access to art history. Not physical access, but emotional access."

I remembered my art history classes in high school. They were excruciatingly boring, even more boring than learning the dead languages that existed before the Unifying Language. "If something is dead, why don't we just bury it and forget about it, like we do with our dead people?" I wondered back then. I spent many evenings struggling through the compulsory novel *Anna Karenina*. Apparently reading *Anna Karenina* used to be some kind of divine experience, but for Guided people it was a frustrating experience of reading about a bunch of unhinged individuals with an extreme lack of self-awareness and very poor decision-making skills. It was like reading a cookbook from before the invention of fire. Therefore, it didn't feel like a huge loss to me at the time that we did not have this emotional access anymore.

"The only thing that disrupts our Guided society now are the UnGuided," the voice-over continued. "Societies of humans who live in little clumps in the forest, refusing to move with the times. Of course, we do not punish the UnGuided. We have Free Will without exceptions. Sadly, the UnGuided are no longer welcome in our public places, since they have made it their goal to disrupt our harmony. Our Guided system is built to make only minor modifications to people's emotional state, because it is not desirable to have everyone act and feel exactly the same. Being exposed to extreme displays of emotions can eventually break through the natural barriers the Guided have built up and cause a state of distress. Feeling distress and panic are uncommon for us, and we are not trained in getting these levels down."

I thought of my old office at the Guided Infrastructure Department, which had tranquilizer darts on hand to take out UnGuided terrorists who staged public disruption interventions. I wondered if they would take me back at the Infrastructure Department. Would I be met with distrust? Would it be uncomfortable? Quickly I reminded myself that distrust and discomfort were UnGuided states. The Infrastructure Department would do just what Jane did, taking me back without hesitation. A faint feeling of regret traveled through my half-Guided body when I thought of her statement "I am willing to take you back."

Would I rather have had her not take me back? I suspected I subconsciously wished for her to create some sort of obstacle for me to overcome. This was the kind of complex UnGuided desires I had been learning about over the last months. The need to be rejected in order to crave the love.

I knew Jane's love was real and strong. She would give a kidney for me if she needed to.

"Sometimes the UnGuided stage their disruptions as positive emotional interventions, like art displays, and sometimes by way of negative emotional interventions, like aggressive displays of feelings. All of this happens with the goal of breaking through people's Guided states and reminding them of the full range of human emotions. When caught, the UnGuided individuals are brought to rehabilitation centers, where they are placed on a mild Guided regimen. We then allow them the choice of going fully Guided or returning to their UnGuided state and being dropped off in the forest. Most of them are relieved to rejoin civilization."

"AGF, stop program," I said. Listening to the program, I felt ashamed (but mildly ashamed, since my Guided probe was doing its work) that I was one of those UnGuided terrorists. It is what brought me to this Guided Facility: I was shot with a tranquilizer dart after haranguing people at a public market, screaming and crying and shouting in their ears. I closed my eyes as I remembered my behavior. And the long braids. Jane must have seen the field footage by now. I pictured her shrugging as she watched it. "It's her Free Will," I imagined her saying to Daisy on her lap.

Many ways

Outside, the sun set behind the skyscrapers, turning the clouds pink. I didn't feel any awe over the color spectacle outside my window. I didn't feel sadness anymore about losing my friends, just a faint sense of appreciation for having had the experience. I did not feel hysterical pain over lost love. No tension. Just a calm steadiness, a vague but very pleasant sensation. The implant in my right thumb had now reached 60 percent. This is what I knew would happen, I was familiar with the experience of being Guided.

And still I was not prepared for it. It seemed as if my recent memories were leaving me, because they were connected to the emotions I had when I was UnGuided. I climbed out of the hospital bed, and with my eyes closed and my legs crossed, I sat down on the floor. Feeling the sides of my feet touch the cold tile, feeling the texture of my hospital gown under my hands, I tried to do the Mental Clarity Exercise we practiced within the UnGuided community. It struck me that the exact state we aimed to achieve by humming and meditating was a natural replica of the Guided state. Why had I not thought of that before?

With my eyes still closed I tried to remember my reasons for joining the UnGuided, but they were drifting further and further away and tied to my disappearing feelings. Why did I join the UnGuided society? How on earth did that happen? At the time I had just moved in with Jane, which was not the big change I thought it would be. Our simple, easy merging predicted a steady life together. I remember sometimes wondering what I could learn about myself if I experienced more friction. I wasn't doubting the Guided system that much; I was just pondering life and the purpose of it all. Jane gave me joy. We had deep conversations, we had fun, we had an active sex life. But when I was walking Daisy through the forest near our cottage, I sometimes tried to remember what I had expected from moving in together and from life altogether.

It was during one of those walks when I stumbled on one of the UnGuided art interventions. This particular one was a dance. Between the oak trees, a group of about fifteen dancers were performing in the silence of the woods, the only sounds coming from them: heavy breathing, feet hitting the ground, bodies rubbing against one another. I can't describe what it evoked in me, seeing these bodies entangling themselves, fighting and embracing and then finally pushing away again.

In the diary I kept during my first weeks after the amputation, I wrote about this experience: "When I saw the performance, feelings started surging through my body, but not only feelings—colors, patterns, memories! Memories of my mother, my father; memories of them holding me as a child, much further back even; memories of humankind, all blending together in a multilayered sea, the universe stretching out inside of me."

Looking back, I knew this was crazy of course: "memories of humankind." But it was powerful. Powerful enough to—can you imagine it!—let go of dear Daisy's leash, who thankfully knew her way back home, and follow the disappearing group.

How to explain it? The same young girl who did her school presentation about the importance of herd harmony, the same woman who was teased at the Infrastructure Department for never ever changing her mind on anything, now went into the wild, leaving behind all that was dear and sane. It pains me to remember I did not think of Jane at all. "It's just for a moment," I had told myself as I followed them. An hour later I was convincing the UnGuided group leader I was ready to join. The thumb with the implant was amputated later that night. During the following days, while I was kept in a hut surrounded by loving chanting and meditators, they arranged for the Letter to be sent to my family, informing them of my decision, assuring them I was all right, and inviting them to join as well. The message was actually written on paper and folded into an envelope, as was once done generations ago. A vast majority of Guided people had only read about such letters in media stories, shaking our heads in disbelief before moving on with our day.

But now I was the culprit. I, Little Miss Perhaps One Day We Can Guide the Animals Toward Civilization Too, had joined the idiots in the forest. It was not easy to live in an outcast society. The practical problems with health care, comfort, and food were stressful. But the general discord, in the group and within myself, was the hardest part and very often overwhelming. First came the expected feelings of panic and loneliness—sometimes missing my family felt like being sawed in half, and I had shameful outbursts of anger over the smallest things, like people breathing loudly through their nostrils. Not long after, I was introduced to my PMS, an emotional monstrosity that seemed manageable at first but quickly revealed itself to be the most destructive, deceptive, and undermining force I'd ever encountered, and one that emanated from my own body. Some people in our group were against all interventions like shampoo and vaccinations, which led to divisions in all kinds of subgroups and the slow terror of endless meetings, with certain subgroup leaders insisting on using dead languages that no one understood.

The reward? I learned the strange layeredness of emotions, like mixing colors. I learned the meaning of individuality. I understood the joy in terrible things, like being selfish, stealing a lover, and screaming at the top of your lungs during an argument, and even the weird freedom that came from getting terribly rejected. All these notes, all these colors, all mine! And I understood bliss.

When Ali, my UnGuided lover, and I took all the honey we gathered from the hives and guzzled it up under the setting sun, without giving anyone else any of it, we felt it. Bliss. The guilt we felt somehow reinforced the sense of bliss. I understood the beauty in imperfection. I believe there should be a new word for this form of beauty and the deep emotion it can evoke. It's not as sparkly as beauty, not as serious and transcendent as Kant's notion of the sublime. It is like suddenly picking up the hum of the universe, or an acute sense of being part of the hum of the universe.

I can't explain it. It's the strongest feeling, the rarest. It's the feeling I had when I stumbled upon the art intervention. I had it a few times more: when I walked out into the cornfield on my own late at night feeling angry with everyone else. I stood under the black sky, and suddenly I felt like everything was all right and I was all right and every single thing that existed fitted together perfectly. I felt it once when we were sitting together after dinner with a small group, laughing at a joke, and I suddenly saw the others—really, really saw them: how they were, how they carried a whole flawed world inside of them, just like me. It happened when I woke up at night and saw my lover sleeping next to me. When I reread *Anna Karenina*. When I stepped into the river and the light played on the surface of the water, and I felt the cold water between my toes and the hot sun on my shoulders.

Those moments were juxtaposed by extreme terror. I learned what it is like to have harm done to you. I learned what it is to do harm. To not be safe in your group. Abuse, panic, murder, bullying, punishment—these abstract concepts from history I now encountered in person, one by one. I saw how one individual can sow immense pain among hundreds of others, just by one action, one small choice. In my Guided life, I had seen children suffer because society had not yet been able to abolish all diseases. But when we saw a child suffer because of the preventable, selfish actions of one individual, even the toughest in our group went to their beds doubting our choice to live UnGuided. And all the meditation in the world did not prevent suicides, which were unheard of in Guided territory but were common in our group. And it seemed to have a contagious effect on others. After what happened to Ali, I became more radical at first. I hated Guided society even more. If it hadn't shut us out the way it did, I reasoned, it would not have made Ali feel like she would never connect with her family again, something she often cried about. It was the Guided state that was to blame. But inside, at a very deep, unreachable level, I doubted what I was doing, just as I had doubted my life with Jane.

When I volunteered for the negative emotional intervention taking place at a public market near my old house, I must have been motivated by this subconscious desire. How better to achieve a return to my old life than by going to my old market, screaming and crying, and practically begging to be shot by the tranquilizer gun? I was the first person in my cell to reject the shuttle back to the forest and accept the offer of a return to Guided life.

My fear that I would be treated with disgust and disparagement by the Guided world when I came back was, of course, unfounded. I now see that this idea was based on my own emotions. My desire to punish and reject people who had hurt me was UnGuided, while the Guided people—my people—have long risen above such damaging interactions. I can still be loved, cared for, accepted. Love is not dependent on pain. Love is not linked to rejection.

It is a relief to be back, feeling myself connected again. I tell myself this now, sitting on the floor, my legs crossed. And at the end of the six weeks in this hospital, I will go back to Jane. I will have to successfully complete the Disruption Test, a notoriously difficult test designed to find out if people are fully Guided again, emotionally but also politically. The test was made to filter out the Undercovers. Only people of a very calm and controlled nature—and I am aware some could claim that I am one of those, and therefore chosen by my community!—could succeed in going undercover in Guided society and retain their UnGuided ideology while plugged into the Guided system, using meditation and willpower. The rumor was that the UnGuided were planting members in Guided society, hoping they would find work at the departments, so they could get to the source of the system and disrupt it. But trust me—I'm not one of those. I have seen enough unnecessary conflict. I have felt enough pain. I am once again the biggest champion of the Guided state.

Yes, there is the loss of occasional bliss. There is the loss too of great culture—those intense novels and indescribable sculptures and dead languages and all that—but it is a small price to pay for happiness. Because in the end, isn't happiness all there is?

Is there anything beyond happiness, really?

The King and His Things

THE KING COUNTED HIS THINGS. As a king, he had a lot of things, and the counting lasted days and weeks and years until, suddenly, the dozing palace was stirred up by his cry. "Must have more things!"

The counting king called a meeting.

"Point number one," he said, "is that I must have more things. Point number two," he continued, "is that I shall behead someone if I don't get more things. And point number three," he concluded, " is that whoever gets me what I haven't already got will be rewarded with a cancellation of decapitation. You, you, you, and you!"

The king pointed out four valets with his baton: a fat one, a skinny one, a handsome one, and an ugly one.

"Shoo!"

The valets ran into the kingdom, their knees shaking with fear. The fat one started his search in the north because that was close by. He arrived at a town just after nightfall, but the only thing he found there was the cold.

"Must eat something first," he said to himself, and he knocked on a little stone shack's door. In the shed he found a dead-frozen family piled up on the floor, but aside from that, the place was empty. The same thing in the next shack and the next shack. It wasn't until the very last one that he found something that resembled life. A small group of people sat curled up in the corner of the shed, blue-faced and shaking.

"Finally!" the valet cried, and lowered himself on the floor with a sigh, using his mink coats as pillows. "I'm a representative of the king. Feed me, please."

A lump of bread was thrown at the valet. Between bites the valet spoke of the terrible things he had endured that day: the moody king, whose yelling had made his ears whistle; the terrible cold, which had made him feel sneezy; the sight of the dead people, which had made him feel nauseated.

Suddenly, one of the creatures in the corner started speaking about the town and the king and the cold. In an unstable voice: "This ice age seems to last for ages . . . And the king has confiscated all the blankets and all the clothes and all the wood and all the matches, leaving the village to freeze to death. The only reason we survived is because we braided this blanket out of the hair of our deceased daughters."

"That's brilliant!" The valet demanded the blanket in the name of the king and traveled back to the palace, where the king was lying snoring in his bedstead.

"King," the valet whispered as he tiptoed into the king's bedroom. "King."

"Go away. I'm sleeping," the king groaned.

The valet kneeled by the bedstead.

"But I have something you don't have," the valet said, and he lifted the blanket above his head.

The king's grumpy face appeared above the edge of the bedstead. "It's a blanket," he said.

"But braided from the hairs of deceased children." The valet smiled, certain that the king did not have that yet.

But the king said, "I've already got that," and he swept his sword so that the head of the valet rolled over the carpet. Then he went back to sleep.

Meanwhile, the skinny valet found a sandy desert wind in the east of the kingdom, a wind so strong it planed all the clothes off his skin. With only two pieces of string left on his body, the valet finally arrived in the eastern capital, where the wind was peculiarly absent.

"How do you keep the wind away?" the valet asked the villagers.

The villagers took him to the border of the town and said, "The king wants to keep all windscreens to himself, which is why every villager gives his firstborn to this living shield."

With a sad look on their faces, they pointed at the row of boys and girls, held together by a large rope, that surrounded the town.

“I’ll take it,” the valet said, and he brought it to the king.

“A windscreen made out of firstborns,” he told the king, but the king already had one, even two, and the skinny valet was done for as well.

Valet number three, the handsome one, went south, where the sun burned. Here too the villagers had thought of ingenious ways to protect themselves from the force of nature. But this valet had heard the stories about valet number one and valet number two and planned to search thoroughly, passing on hats made of human skin, not even looking twice at shades made out of bones. He traveled all the way to the southernmost corner of the empire. Here he found a farmer, who was sitting on the ground, crying, a wooden object balanced on his head.

“Excuse me,” the valet said from under his parasol, “but what is that on your head?”

The farmer spoke about the king, who wanted all the shade for himself, confiscated all the parasols and trees, et cetera et cetera. “They took every bit of my house, I could only rescue this piece of wood, which I use to keep my scalp from setting fire. I have hit three nails in it, to keep it in place on my head.”

“Excellent,” the valet whispered. “That simple.”

He grabbed the thing off the farmer’s head and ran back to the palace. He laughed as he yelled, “King! Here it is! A piece of wood with three nails in it! Something you surely don’t have!”

But the king didn't smile. He said, "Idiot! That was the first thing I had!"

The valet got smacked with the wood and with an axe in his neck.

Now for the last valet standing. Number four, the ugly valet, had been in the completely flooded west for a while. Shocked, he floated around town in his rubber boat. The people here had cut off their own limbs and tied them tightly together to use as rafts! With tears in his eyes, he asked a man passing by what had happened. The man, no more than a torso, told the valet about the king who kept all the boats and rafts in the royal pond and confiscated all the wood. He told him about the hot south, the windy east, and the cold north. He concluded his story with the terrible fate of the three other valets.

"Give it up," he said. "You're going down too. The king has confiscated every single thing in the world."

Hereupon, the fourth valet returned to the palace. With empty hands he faced the king, who giggled and screamed: "Tell me I have everything! I have every single thing there is!"

The king reached for his sword, but the valet spoke: "No, King. You do not have everything. What you do not have is a good heart."

The king fell silent. Tears welled up in his eyes as he stood up from his throne.

"You're right," he said. "That I haven't got. You won't be beheaded."

Solemnly, the king walked up to the valet. He cut open the valet's chest with the sword and took out his good heart. Carefully, he added it to his collection and started counting again.

Für Elise

ELISE WAS A promising young girl. She started playing the flute when she was three years old, moving on to the violin when her grandmother gave her one for her seventh birthday. At nine, she could flawlessly play Simeon ten Holt's Capriccio for Solo Violin, but her family most appreciated her for playing "Für Elise." Every birthday party, every wedding, she was asked to play "Für Elise"—her own name and the name of her grandmother.

Above her desk Elise had pictures of musicians who had inspired her, people who had played or created beautiful pieces that touched her.

"My talented sister," her older brother said. Her older sister told her friends how Elise could play "How Deep Is Your Love" by the Bee Gees on her violin after listening to it only once on the radio. As much as her family bragged about her and celebrated her talent, there was not much room for practice. With her older sister getting pregnant at seventeen and her brother developing a habit of getting into trouble all the time, she was the one her mother leaned on.

After school, Elise came home to care for her grandmother, as her mother started her shift in the family restaurant. She cleaned the house, got the groceries, cooked, had dinner with Grandma. She played the violin at school. A music teacher let her use the band's practice space during breaks. And this teacher wrote a special note to Elise's parents, recommending that Elise apply to music school.

Elise's parents did not have much time to reflect on the note. Her father's back got worse during her final year in high school, and it was decided that her mother had to run the restaurant. During the summer after Elise's graduation, Elise's sister had a miscarriage, and Elise was asked to help out in the restaurant during the lunch hours, as her mother helped her sister with the children. Elise did so gladly, because she was not only talented but also very sensitive. She did not know what it was like to have a miscarriage, but the deep sadness carried by her sister came through very clear to her, like the dull thumping of the timpani.

The last call to apply for music school was missed that year, but when the time came to apply for music school again the following year, she did it. And she got through the first round. "Sublime accents, a natural," one of the teachers on the admissions committee had said.

On the train back, Elise kept turning that sentence over and over in her head. "Sublime accents, a natural." A letter came to the house a few days later: the official invitation for the second round of auditions. It was an entire week of master classes and performances, costing over $500. Elise's father opened the letter while she was at the restaurant. And when she came home she found out he had called the school and shouted at the administrator. Why should the parents cover the costs of the auditions and a hotel? The school should do it, her father said. It is a scam.

As a tear-filled fight erupted in the house, it became clear that there was a bigger problem. The family funds were not there. Her sister's wedding had cost a lot, her parents had needed some, and her brother had cleared the rest. Even the money her grandmother had set aside for Elise's music career was not completely there anymore after the roof of the restaurant started leaking.

The money for the week in Vancouver Elise could have paid from her own savings, but there was no way she could afford the tuition of nearly $20,000 a year. The forms required for grant applications confused her, they were so complicated. Where was she going to get five letters of recommendation? Why didn't she think of the money before?

Instead of going to the second round of auditions, Elise decided to save her money and work another year in the restaurant. She worked six days a week in the kitchen and cared for her grandmother in the evenings. Sometimes her parents needed part of her salary to pay the rent. It was only fair, Elise thought, since she still lived at home and did not pay any rent. A thing that bothered her more was that it was unclear how her mother would manage to care for both her grandmother and the restaurant when Elise left. It was never discussed.

Her father, who couldn't work at all anymore because of his back, spent most of his time in the coffeehouse. Of course he could care for his mother-in-law, but it was wrong to ask him to wash a woman's hair, to put on her stockings. Already his ego was damaged, with his wife running his business for him. Elise felt that she could hear the sound of her father's damaged self-image every time she came close to it. An alarming, high-pitched clarinet. If his daughter challenged him, questioned his health situation, suggested that he do women's work, she did not know what he would do.

Telling no one, Elise took the train to Vancouver that winter. She went to audition for a famous orchestra. It would take in three young prodigies, the ad had said. In the waiting room she found she was much older than the other candidates. Her face was bright red as she waited among the parents with their child prodigies. She watched how these parents were encouraging them, cleaning their bows, and adjusting their collars. She felt ancient. And indeed she was turned away, because the audience wanted to see brilliant children, not twenty-year-olds. "Unparalleled, remarkable talent," the conductor said, whose eyes had gotten shiny as she played. He squeezed her hands as he repeated, "Keep going, keep going."

The next audition for music school took place in the week her father announced he wanted to divorce her mother. He was going to marry someone else. They already had an apartment together, he and the new fiancée, with his name etched in marble in the apartment lobby. Elise had seen this sign. She went along with her brother to keep him calm as he conducted a furious investigation into his father's second life. Her mother had a mental breakdown, her sister took her mother to a clinic, and Elise babysat the kids as their grandfather's long-running lies were revealed one by one in the following weeks.

She did not even mention the audition for music school this time. Her family seemed to have forgotten about her unparalleled talent, except at birthdays and weddings, when she was asked to play "Für Elise." She began avoiding the gazes of the people in the frames above her bed.

Four years went by, and something inside her said it was too late, so she skipped auditions without even trying to make them work. A childhood friend had already graduated from music school and was now working as a part-time waiter, playing flute in an orchestra some nights.

More years passed, and Elise worked in the restaurant and spent time with her grandmother and mother. It went well. She had a talent for music and a talent for caring.

Later, when her nieces were older, when her grandmother had died and her mother had seamlessly slipped into the role of patient, Elise thought of reigniting her violin practice. She took lessons, but she was better than the teacher. They soon spent their time together just hanging out, talking about music. Elise showed her teacher better thumb positioning and talked about how she heard music in everyone she met, in the forests, and in the clouds and the flowers. She shared how frustrating it was that no one else seemed to hear it. In turn, the teacher spoke of her violent marriage, something Elise had sensed in every note she played.

With her family, Elise grew distant.

When they all exchanged long hugs or loving words at the end of a family gathering, Elise remained silent and stood rigid in their embrace. Because she knew her sister wasn't available when her mother fell ill, she knew her brother avoided phone calls when her mother had fallen down the stairs again, she knew how far their love truly reached when things got difficult. It was not as far as they conveyed in those loving words exchanged in the doorway.

Elise got a reputation for being cold.

On the rare occasions she displayed her emotions it was volcanic, unexpected, and traumatic for those around her.

"Play us 'Für Elise,'" her brother said on the seventy-fifth birthday party for her mother. Elise declined. She was not in the mood. Her violin teacher had left; she had finally gotten out of the bad marriage and moved to Mexico. An email from her was waiting in Elise's inbox. A tiny icon of an unopened envelope with the subject "Found an orchestra!" that she could not bring herself to click on.

Urged on by her family to play "Für Elise," she explained, "I need to change the strings, the sound is dull."

"We won't hear it," her brother said. He was eager to impress his new fiancée. Like his father, he had gotten engaged to a new woman while still married to his first wife. Still, he refused to forgive him. "Come on." He turned to his fiancée. "She could play any song she heard on the radio after just one listen."

"Remember 'How Deep Is Your Love'?" her sister said.

"The Bee Gees!" Her brother laughed.

"Who are the Beegees?" the new fiancée asked.

"I'm going to get the cake," Elise said. She got up from the sofa.

"Just play 'Für Elise,'" her brother pressed. "It would mean a lot to Mum too." He nodded at their mother, who was falling asleep in her chair.

"It's called 'Für Elise,'" Elise said slowly. "That means 'for Elise.'" She could hear her voice change. "For me."

Inside of her something was happening. An emotional rupture, worse than times before. This one resembled the fourth movement of Eugène Ysaÿe's Sonata no. 2. Abrupt, slashing bow strokes.

"For me," Elise repeated to her family. "For me. Do you even understand what I mean by that?"

"I just thought it would be—" her brother said.

"But it never is for me," Elise interrupted, "is it? It is always for someone else. Someone who wants this. Wants that.

Wants more. More. More." She was yelling a little bit. The room was silent. Her mother had woken up.

The brother, putting his arm around their mother, said, "I don't know where this is coming from."

"If you were ever unhappy, or if we have over-asked you, you should have let us know," the sister said.

"If you have over-asked me," Elise said. "If you have over-used me. How can you not know?" A sob tried to work its way up to her throat, but she did not let it. Instead she turned to her brother: "When you yelled at me because the driving gloves you want to wear for your second stupid wedding were the wrong color! And you kept texting me about it, how I had to order new ones through my account, even though I was taking Mother to the hospital."

She turned to her sister: "When you asked me to babysit for an emergency. On my only day off. And it turns out it's for a bachelorette party. When you wanted, begged, demanded to have a new car, and you asked me to ask Mum to lend you the money because she already said no to you. Do you know what that was like for me? You want, want, want, always more, more, more. And now you are asking me to let you know when you over-ask. I have to do that work as well."

It was quiet in the room. Then her sister got up. "Oh, Ellie," she said, tears on her cheeks. "I am sorry." She walked up to Elise and embraced her.

The moment was real, as light and simple as the first notes of "Für Elise" itself.

Then Elise made a mistake. She accepted the embrace and began crying. She softened in her sister's arms. Knowing immediately she had wasted her rage, she cried more. The moment was lost. She accepted the understanding and apologies that came her way. They would not call her about the wedding again, sorry. Most of the money for the car had already been paid back, did she know? They would try to help her cover some of the hospital appointments, but frankly, with the children, if she knew what it was like to be a parent . . .

Elise tolerated their reassurances, knowing that in the end, this had nothing to do with them.

Her life was her fault and her fault alone.

She played "Für Elise," and they applauded.

And her brother and sister had taken note of her outburst. The topics of wedding outfits, loans, and babysitting were not mentioned for several months. Her brother's fiancée became slightly scared of her.

So Elise gained a reputation for being "complicated," "unpredictable." A strange reputation for the only person who was always there and could be counted on, she felt. On the day she turned fifty-five, she decided to stop her outbursts and accept her life. When she sat by her mother's side, holding her hand, she could feel the emotions in her like a symphony, and she could dip into the soft, gentle waves of the cellos. She felt beautiful music when she was with her sister's children too, an easy triangle. Caring is not a wasted life.

When Elise died at sixty-seven there was no God waiting for her, no afterlife. No one put her picture up above their desks, because she had only cared, and those who care for others are rarely remembered. She played the violin very well but never took it further than that. Her brother told the story of the Bee Gees song at the funeral. Her sister told several misremembered anecdotes about their strong connection. They did not play "Für Elise"—somehow, finally, they understood.

An alternative ending for Elise

"Oh, Ellie," her sister said, tears on her cheeks. "I am sorry."

But Elise raised her hands to keep her sister from embracing her. She knew all too well how this would go if she allowed herself to soften. The crying, the apologies, the misplaced understanding. She would end up playing "Für Elise" again.

So she did not allow them to comfort her. Instead she took her violin and her handbag and got in her car. She drove to a hotel. It was then she opened the email from her violin teacher. With her phone on silent, Elise started looking for plane tickets, ignoring all the calls that came in, not even answering a message asking where her mother's heart medication could be found.

After booking a plane ticket, Elise took the violin and played, to herself, "Für Elise." It was her finest rendition; the flatness that had entered her playing was gone and replaced with a new kind of compassion in the low notes and a mild, almost cheerful anger in the higher register.

The next day she got on a plane to Mexico City, where she rented a car and drove to the city where her violin teacher had rented an Airbnb apartment. She introduced Elise to the local orchestra where she played. They needed a conductor. It was funded by an elderly couple who hosted recitals for the town every month. It paid very little. Elise started giving music lessons to expats and did music projects at the local international school. Coupled with her savings, it worked. Not everyone in the orchestra was equally talented, but all the players were ambitious, present, and open to her leadership.

Elise's family called one by one as the news of her move spread, some with accusations, some with questions, others to just talk about themselves.

"We have put all your belongings in storage," her sister wrote in a cold text.

Her brother sent her the bill for the storage unit, which she paid.

It did not take long for her mother to deteriorate. A few months later, as reported by her brother, they discovered her lying on the floor. She had fallen on her way to the toilet in the middle of the night, managed to crawl to the living room, but could not reach the phone. She had soiled herself and was barely conscious when they found her. He sent a photo of it: her mother, yellowish and gaunt, on the carpet.

"Since you left," he captioned the photo.

Elise replied. She agreed it was her fault for leaving and that she was very sad. That was it.

A new life had opened up, easily, as if thousands of potential lives had always been waiting for her, like envelopes waiting to be opened.

When Elise died at sixty-seven there was no God waiting for her, no afterlife. No one put her picture up above their beds. The orchestra played a concert in her honor, and the children at school painted her violin and hung it above the entrance of the music room.

The Monsters Outside the Village

THE MONSTERS OUTSIDE the village hadn't always been there. In old village journals a time was described that was simpler. A time when there were no monsters, nothing to see out the window, nothing to feed, nothing to worship, nothing to detest. There were only two Miracles known back then: the Miracle Birth of the son of Jan Heek to his widow, Jannie, that happened eleven months after his death, and the Miracle of the Healing Well, the well with medicinal qualities that appeared in the cow field. Before the Miracle of the Monsters occurred, the life of the villagers consisted of just their families and their houses, their fields, their trapping and fishing, winter and spring, summer and autumn. It was a simpler life, idyllic maybe, but the villagers of today didn't want this empty existence. Life with the monsters is what they knew.

It all started long ago when a woman named Hendrikje went out to a clearing by the river, just outside the village gates. She had kept a diary for many years. In this diary she mainly chronicled unpleasant arguments she had with her mother, but now that she and her mother had made peace, she wanted the diary to be gone. Near the oak tree that the villagers called "Donar's Oak," she built a small pillar of old moss, leaves, and broken branches and set the diary on fire.

At first, Hendrikje told no one what strange and unsettling things had happened in the moments that followed the diary being set on fire. She told no one how the smoke that curled up from the fire had turned into a giant translucent figure—a monster, really—that rose high above her. She gasped as she recognized it. The monster had taken the shape of Hendrikje's mother, crawling on her hands and knees, looking for the glasses that she had recently thrown at Hendrikje in a rage—exactly as was described on page thirteen of her diary. Hendrikje told no one that she had then ran to the well, holding her breath so as not to inhale any of the monstrous smoke, and filled a bucket of medicine water to throw on the fire, and with the fire the monster also died down.

The next day, at sunrise, Hendrikje went back to the clearing by the river to find out if what had happened had really been true. She brought with her a letter to her mother. She had written it during the night, and it was full of doodles of hearts and flowers, words of understanding and praise, and the promise not to give her father beer anymore. She set it on fire. Again, a monster rose from the flames. This time it was even more spectacular than the last. The monster that came into being from the smoke was pink, purple, and red, and it transformed into the shape of two figures, one big and one small, dancing across the sky. Hendrikje, who could only hold her breath for so long, finally inhaled the smoke, discovering that it made her feel clear on the inside, like the air on a winter morning. Adding some more moss on the fire, her monster grew bigger. Above the village the monster did an hourlong dance of shapes and colors that showed Hendrikje's renewed relationship with her mother, displayed in fantastical detail, until the fire died and it disappeared again.

When curious villagers started wandering out the town's gates to find the source of the smoky monster, Hendrikje was relieved. The reason she hadn't told anyone was because she'd been concerned she'd be like her childhood friend Bertha, who had been put in a bed in a hospital in Uld-Heske for two years because she claimed the trees in the forest told her what to do. But this monster wasn't a figment of Hendrikje's imagination. The others saw it too. And they accepted it instantly as the Third Miracle of the village: the Miracle of the Monster. No one questioned why it had appeared, because they also did not know why the stars in the sky appeared each night, or why the pale female ghosts lured drunk men into the forest after midnight, or where dreams came from. They did not even know how or why they themselves had come to exist. There was only the question of what to do next.

"There is only the question of what to do next," Hendrikje announced, and she sent the villagers to their houses to find more letters and images to burn.

The first one to try the monster was Annie, the village carpenter. She chose to burn the design she made for a rebuilding of the village's water mill, which the village had voted against. As soon as her designs caught fire, the monster rose up and built her mill in the sky. It was just as she designed it, except more magnificent. Annie felt fulfilled and thrilled by the sight of the majestic wings sweeping over the village. Suddenly her design no longer just existed in her head and on measly papers that no one looked at long enough to fully understand them, but in real life, for all to see. All the insecurities she had about her talent disappeared in an instant. As she inhaled the monster's smoke, her chest rose with pride at who she saw herself becoming.

Hendrikje, who thought herself the village leader where the monster was concerned, wanted to do more experiments. She asked a group of villagers to bring some books from the library. What would the monster do with them? Together they set fire to fourteen books from the village library, and the monster roared from the flames again. Hooves and tongues and udders were formed from the pages of *The Encyclopedia of Cattle Breads* (second edition), turning to deep purple spheres that resembled swaying feminine hips and beetroot when *The Literary Review for Rural Women* caught fire, transforming to a magnificent flaxen cabinet that must have come from *Woodworking with Spruce*. The giant spruce box enveloped the entire village for a moment, and everybody was captured inside of it. The villagers stopped their work, the digging up of the potatoes, the peeling of the onions, the kissing of their children, everything, and looked up at the sky to watch the mesmerizing display. This day was now officially the birthday of the monster. The monster's smoke seeped into the villagers' lungs and into their veins. Everyone felt stimulated and alive.

This time, they did not let the fire go out. Villagers kept feeding images and stories, ideas and memories, to the fire, and they saw their lives and hearts transformed into the glorious spectacles they always knew they should be. Some of the villagers did not want their memories, ideas, and images to merge with the others in one great conflagration. They wanted their own moment with the monster. Lines started to form; schedules were made diligently by Hendrikje and, later, by the mayor herself. For instance, between 10:00 and 11:00 it would be farmer Jakob's time with the monster. He burned a copy of his predictions for his acres: careful calculations on what to sow where and for how many years, and which fruit tree should follow the other. The monster became the shape of branches filled with grapes and peaches, wild and lustrous, and these branches encircled the village as a coil for an hour. Jakob beamed with pride as the villagers cheered and toasted to his harvest.

Eleven villagers later, the cobbler Stien burned a page describing her dream of having a baby. The monster displayed such a harmonious vision of Stien holding a baby with round red cheeks much like her own that a quarrel broke out when the next villager tried to take their turn with the monster.

"Don't destroy my baby," Stien pleaded, and since everyone knew she had lost two babies prematurely and once walked into the freezing river out of grief, they kept her fire undisturbed and simply carried a piece of the fire elsewhere to continue it.

So, the monster multiplied into as many monsters as there were villagers, trails of smoke climbing into the sky alongside one another, until there was a wall of colored monster smoke around the village.

Soon the villagers found different ways to make use of the monsters. When a new mayor needed to be elected, all the candidates were asked to use the monster to demonstrate their plans. When their best drawings and most beautiful descriptions were swallowed by the monster's fire, their dreams for the village rose high above the buildings for all to see.

A happy and organized village was proposed by mayoral candidate Harm, the trader. His monster was a tempting display of productivity and collaboration, depicting everyone smiling, a much shorter line at Pelle the butcher's, unclogged sewers, clean water coming through pipes into every house, and each person wearing a beautiful woolen coat.

A village festive and bright, with not two but twelve yearly dance feasts, was what Geertruida the gardener offered. She had created the most colorful monster, made even more spectacular by using wood from the old chestnut tree that she had chopped down just for the occasion.

The wooden bridge reinforced and the streetlights repaired—that was the vision offered by the current mayor. She generated just a little monster, because she did not want to spend too much of the tight village budget on burning wood.

When the village inevitably voted for Harm and his vision of everyone prosperous and smiling, Harm purchased five wheelbarrows' worth of wood to throw onto his fire, which turned into a blazing display. Everyone smiled as they gazed up, his monster's first promise coming true.

Well, not everyone smiled. There were a few villagers who objected to the monsters and who sat alone inside their homes on nights like those. They could not join in when everyone was talking about it the next day. But the minute they changed their minds and decided to start their own monster, everyone embraced them and brought them some paper and wood. Soon, every little girl and boy who was born received their own fire and little monster. The fire was maintained by their parents until they were old enough to take over.

Keeping the monsters going all day and all night meant the village was permanently blanketed in a colorful haze, constantly filled with images and forms that mirrored their lives in ways they preferred. Sometimes the villagers would draw pictures of what the monster had created and put those back in the fire; sometimes they did this many times over, and then they tried to mimic what the monster had shown them down on the ground. This launched many new fashions, interactions, and facial expressions in the village, though none of it looked as good as it did in the sky.

Trading changed too. Houses on the outer ring of the village got more in demand, because who wouldn't want to watch their monster from the window? Adding beautiful drawings or engravings, spectacular phrases, stanzas of poetry, and premium wood created the best monsters, and those with the means purchased fine books to tear pages from, elegant prints, and rare woods, all of which made their monster unique. Timber harvesting, bookselling, papermaking, illustration, painting, and engraving soon became the most important trades in the village.

When the artist Willem proposed to the butcher's daughter Annetje, his monster proposal rose so high into the sky that a contingent from distant Uld-Heske came on horseback to join in the celebrations. Annetje was so proud she forgot Willem was a friend of her father's who was twenty years older than her. She and Willem merged their monsters into one. In the years after, it gave her peace to know her monster was taken care of, even when she was lying in the cold marriage bed while he worked late in his workshop; it soothed her that from her bedroom window she could see their monster displayed, high above everyone else's, telling a continuous tale of passionate love.

The generations that followed grew up with the monsters, it was what they knew. They started and ended their work with a walk to the monsters, under the blinking village lights, over the dislodged slippery bridge; they tended to their monsters and studied their own selves displayed in the sky. On difficult days, when they did not get around to sharpening their knives or when they tripped over the never-finished water pipes that lay discarded in the village square, they found relief in nudging their monster just a tiny bit higher with some old moss and spruce.

Of course, sometimes a nosy child would raise their voice, a voice tiny but clear as a bell, asking, "Why do we have to go to the monsters? We are so tired of it, it is taking too much time. If we are keeping them and feeding them, then can't we also . . . make them go away?"

"No," the villagers would reply anxiously. "Maybe yes, in theory, but no."

"Why would we?" one villager might say if they felt like giving the child an explanation. "No other village even has a monster . . . It gives us joy . . . and we have invested a lot."

"Who says we have the right to kill them?" another might say. "I created my own son and I feed him, but that does not mean I can kill him."

Maybe the child, if it was a persistent one, would then mumble, "But a child has a mind and the monsters do not . . ."

Luckily someone would then finally end this by saying something like, "Doesn't your mother live from the wood trade? Do you want her to lose her work?" and that would be enough to shut the child up.

Now, the villagers weren't stupid. They knew it was exhausting to live with the monsters, who created all sorts of problems in their lives. And, of course, the monsters would shrink and disappear when the fires went out, as they had experienced during the terrifying Three-Day Rain a decade ago. But they could not let the monsters die, they were one with the monsters and they would not exist fully without them. The baby of Stien, for instance, had lived an entire life in the monster, having its own babies and even a death and a funeral, making Stien's life fuller and more real than it could ever have been otherwise. It was them and the monsters, intertwined. That was life now.

If this great multicolored drape was pulled from the village, what would be left?

The Last Inventor

1. The last inventor was a woman, like the first inventor.

2. The last invention determined the path the particles in the universe would take, like the first invention.

3. The last inventor was born in 2062 and called Baby Jameson, the name Baby being very popular in the 2060s. Baby Jameson was a smart and sensitive child. She was the kind of child that noticed everything and therefore quickly developed a contempt of adults, her parents in particular. She despised the uncontrolled way they sparked emotional reactions in each other, without any understanding of where these emotions came from and where they would lead. The despair and rage that filled the house frightened her. By the time she was five years old, Baby had learned to predict and derail her parents' collisions. She blocked holo-calls from her grandmother when her mother was unstable. She asked her father dumb questions so he could explain things when she saw his anger was mounting—this was revealed by the

number of times he touched his eyebrow. Baby even saved up good news to announce during particularly bad days, like the time her father threw a wineglass at her mother. Stepping onto the dining table, Baby announced that she had taught herself French. She then recited the first chapter of Sartre's *Le Mur*.

4. When Baby Jameson was seven years old she gave up on her parents. She spent a lot of time playing old-fashioned games in her grandma's house.

5. The game of chess—with its calculation of future reactions to her own actions—soon obsessed her.

6. Baby Jameson's ability to concentrate deeply and her talent for envisioning and remembering possibility trees, combined with her preference for closed, predictable environments, led to her becoming a chess prodigy. She joined an online chess club and played matches, but it was in real-life competitions that she really excelled. There were other child geniuses who could calculate the possible responses to chess moves at a very high speed, but Baby had one more talent: she was able to analyze and predict the moves of her opponents by studying their emotional tells. How does he place a piece back down on the board after lifting it? Is there a slight tremble? How firmly does her hand grip the pawn? How fast are his eyes moving as he is scanning the board?

7. At ten years old, Baby Jameson played her first National Youth Chess Competition. She used her opponent's

contempt of girls by mimicking nerves and opening with the laughable scholar's mate, while she quietly prepared her attack on the other side of the board. When her opponent captured her queen and she saw him exchange a smile with his father, she knew he had allowed himself to think of her as clueless. Without hesitation, Baby set up a simple trap that opened up the possibility to slide her rook behind his pawns. Checkmate. She became National Youth Champion 2072.

8. That same year she watched her parents divorce. She watched the predictable moves they made to hurt each other. Because they played the game so badly, she lost all respect for them. At fourteen, Baby Jameson moved into her chess coach's beachside apartment.

9. In 2090 Baby Jameson became the first female world champion, after which she retired from chess. She refused to play the computer.

10. Fifteen years later Baby Jameson led the research team at World Institute of Technology (WIT, formerly MIT) in analyzing the game tree of chess. Baby's team reduced the number of possible sensible games by creating a new variation on null-move pruning in heuristic programming and coupled this with new technology based on breakthroughs in data storage for atomic and quantum computing. "When played perfectly on both sides," they announced, "the game of chess is fundamentally a draw."

11. As predictable as this outcome was to Baby Jameson—checkers had already been solved way back in 2007 and it

was also a draw—so unexpected was the kiss from Ezza, the leader of her technical team. This kiss arrived on her lips the night they were awarded the Quantum Prize. For once, she had not seen something coming. It was the beginning of a period of intense happiness. During the day Baby and Ezza worked on possibility trees in games and systems—predicting the weather, patterns in social behaviors, sales trends, and virus outbreaks—while by night they experienced the sweetest thing in life: not-alone-ness.

12. Their relationship lasted almost two years. For Baby Jameson, the unpredictability of Ezza's emotions became unbearable, while for him her compulsion to try to predict and influence his behavior was condescending. "If you manipulate me to be who you want," he said, "you're kissing the mirror." The panic she felt when they fought made her understand for the first time the wild helplessness she had seen in her parents. The day she screamed at him for the first time, she broke up with him.

13. Two months after the breakup, Baby Jameson was the victim of a virus attack on WIT by the Analog Anarchist Group, a bunch of hippies who believed science had ruined the planet, which wasn't true—people had done that. They had contaminated the coffee cups in the lab with a neurovirus that replicated so fast her hand was already numb by the time she put down her cup. Despite her quick administering of a virus blocker, her nervous system was severely damaged, and her recovery took place in quarantine, while

doctors searched for a way to destroy the dormant virus that was still inside of her.

14. Confined to a sterile hospital room with robotic help, Baby Jameson received the news that her grandmother had died. For days she sat in her bed, unable to move, talk, or cry. Her physical pain matched her emotional pain, and she was going over and over the steps she had taken in her life, other steps she could have taken, other outcomes she could have ensured.

15. Baby Jameson became hypersensitive to the smallest unexpected deviations from routine. From her hospital bed she had access to her WIT computing power, which she wasted on tracing and predicting the movement patterns of a spider in the corner of her room, and she was only able to rest when she had accurately calculated and predicted all its future movements.

16. When Baby Jameson was finally free of the virus, she found herself hesitant to leave the facility. The idea was daunting, to dive back into the sea of possibilities and emotional damage that the outside world promised, until an old lab friend reminded her it was not a sea but a tree. "Love, friendship, family, colleagues, any interaction," she said, "isn't that just reaction to action, based on the parameters of each entity?"

Baby shook her head: "There are too many factors. Then there's quantum noise, the uncertainty principle. And you can never perfectly model a system that includes yourself.

Not even theoretically." She looked out the window: magnetic cars were driving in a linked lane down below through the street. She could not help but wonder:

17. If you could predict the most likely outcome of every decision—by calculating the reactions of every person and object in a sealed system—could you push the probabilities high enough to avoid all disappointment, pain, humiliation?

Was it possible to play a perfect game of life?

18. Developments in mapping cell history had made it possible to upload information stored in each cell, spurring huge investments in data storage. Prediction algorithms for human behavior had become very precise since the third pandemic of 2053, when the government gained full access to each citizen's health and mobility data.

19. The experiment of solving life had to take place in an environment where the influence of cosmic and natural factors was radically limited. Under the guise of developing a new prediction tool for the stock market, Baby Jameson collected investments, subsidies, and grants for her project: a closed environment where she would predict human interactions. With the three least inquisitive team members of her WIT group, she moved to a closed-off compound in Panama, where the world's largest underwater computing power station was lodged.

20. Baby Jameson worked on collecting and combining all the information available from every entity in the compound. The compound was clinically sterile and free of insects, the

energy supply was monitored, and they had already solved weather prediction years ago. It was the humans that were by far the most erratic element, since all their behaviors were connected to their psychological state and often conflicted with logic. Baby convinced her team to sync with a deep learning program that monitored everything, from the slightest sound, to a change in body temperature, to the microbes in their gut. As she started linking their data and tracing their influences on each other, the deep learning program quickly picked up on patterns in the most suppressed or hidden behaviors, and the predictions became terrifyingly accurate. Every tense moment, every held breath, every eruption of laughter, was born from a previous moment. It seemed that unseen fluctuations and uncertainties did not need to be fully understood and precisely measured, because they could be charted in terms of likelihoods. Baby became more and more convinced that the future was contained in history after all.

21. She began experimenting with diverting from her own predicted behavior. The system quickly picked up on it and started predicting that too. The resulting feedback loop error nearly collapsed the whole system, but was fixed by a built-in delay and reboot.

22. As the team got closer to completing the data on themselves and the lab, they started to become suspicious about the algorithm, which they nicknamed "the Demon." They worried about the state of mind of their team leader, who had developed a weird habit of surprising team members to see

how they would react. The team staged an intervention just before Christmas, as predicted. Baby Jameson listened to their worries, suggested menopause was making her erratic, and offered them free first-class tickets home for Christmas. They all took the chance to see their families, as she knew they would. Baby then sent a letter to Ezza, saying she was sorry, that she had learned about herself, and that he should come to Panama and spend a week with her, just to talk. Hadn't they done their best work together? She signed off with "I need you," which she knew would do the trick.

23. On the night of December 25, Baby Jameson looked at her creation, the Demon. Fifteen monitors showed the ever-changing statistics and predictions of all the movements inside the compound. She couldn't believe it: every single breath she took, every word she called out, every movement she made, it was all mapped out right before it happened, no matter how unpredictable and random she tried to be. She watched the system predict the twitch in her left eye, followed by a memory of her father resurfacing, followed by a tightening in her chest, followed by a wave of calm caused by seeing the ongoing stream of metrics on the fifteen monitors—the information she needed to avoid any pain that lay ahead. She thought of what Ezza had said: "One day you will realize it's the dance with the unpredictable that makes your life, or any life, beautiful, and if you seek to control everything you will become deeply sick and suspicious of yourself."

He was wrong about that too.

24. She knew now that scientific predestination was true: all inventions that would be made—the mistakes, the articles, the ideas, everything—was already written in the first moments of the universe, each step leading to the next. Wouldn't it be beautiful to dance with that? To lead, even? Today she would be the first person, the first anything, to intentionally deviate from cosmic choreography and change the story. There was no guilt around this. If everything was predetermined, this deviation was too.

Then the buzzer of the entrance door sounded. The camera showed Ezza crossing the threshold of the compound. Up in the sky, it seemed like the stars blinked. Was there a rumble? Quite possibly there was a rumble. In this final moment of this specific universe, Baby thought of herself as a little girl, sitting in that game room with her grandmother, discovering chess.

The Ones and the Others

The people of the Ones lived on a mountain. There were several thousand of them, and they had built their houses against the mountainside. Across their mountain stood another mountain that blocked the wind. In between lay the factories where they manufactured steel for their machines, wood for their homes, and glass for their windows and their microscopes. They made very good microscopes—every One owned several, and every child knew how to use a lens and knew what enormous worlds of detail lay hidden in every leaf, every insect, every drop of spit.

Every day, the chimney pipes of the factories filled the valley of the Ones with their smoke.

"What's that over there beyond the mountain that normally blocks the wind?" One said on a completely clear night, which was an extremely unusual occurrence. Across the valley, beyond the high factory chimneys, past the mountains, beyond the distant mountains, beyond the lake behind the mountains even, it seemed like a little light was burning. The Ones climbed to the top of their mountain and moved around nervously.

"What is that light in the distance? Is that an Other?" They squeezed their eyes as they looked into the distance.

"There are more of them," One of the Ones said. And, yes, as they stared long in the distance, more specks of light emerged.

"Is every speck a little house?"

They tried to count the lights, but there were too many.

"Why do they keep their lights burning till late? What are they up to?" the Ones wondered.

It made the Ones very nervous, and One of them lamented: "Why must there be Others? Why can't there just be Ones? Everything was good when it was just us."

"We will keep an eye on the Others," the Ones concluded.

They positioned someone on top of the mountain permanently to stare into the distance. The lights of the Others could be seen only at night, but usually there was so much smoke that nothing could be seen. It was only on those rare occasions when the wind turned and the smoke cleared that the specks of light appeared again, but they were extremely far away. The Ones squinted, desperately trying to peer into the distance until their eyes hurt.

And that's how the Eye came to be.

The Eye was invented to be the opposite of their microscopes. Instead of looking at something small and very close up, the Eye could help them see things that were very far,

far away. Soon plans were drawn up and a building site was chosen. With all the wood they could harvest from the forest and all the steel they could manufacture in the factory, with all their expertise and skill, they built the Eye—a kind of inverted microscope on an enormous extendable arm that they kept extending farther and farther into the distance. On their end, in the village, the Ones projected what could be seen through the Eye on a large screen. The great creaking telescoping arm of the Eye pressed up and out through the smoke and clouds, over the distant mountain peaks, and across lakes and plains, but the lights of the Others remained distant. The Ones spent countless months, perhaps even many years, relentlessly extending and extending the Eye into the atmosphere, the stratosphere, across a distance so huge that it could not be fathomed, a distance that no one could ever have dreamed to cross, a distance so great that even thinking of it made the Ones feel exhausted. But the Ones kept on building. Until one day, the Others came into sight.

As the little houses of the Others appeared on the screen, all the Ones were summoned, and they gathered around the Eye. With a meticulously developed steering mechanism, they could turn the Eye carefully—which was not easy at this astronomical distance—and spy on the Others. Silently, they let the Eye glide between the houses of the Others that stood on their extremely distant mountain. They learned that the Others manufactured wood and metal, that there were thousands of them, that they sometimes yelled at each other, and that they had horrible habits when they thought they were alone.

Watching the Others—that's how the Ones spent their evenings from then on, sitting on rows of pillows in a large chamber they had built around the Eye, steering it from house to house, disgusted by the bedroom habits of the Others, frightened by their fighting, intimidated by their constant need to eat, sleep, and bother each other.

During the day, they took turns watching the Others too. They felt like it was important to do this, especially since they had recently noticed Others dragging wood and metal to the top of their mountain and building something, some sort of object that leaped out over their valley a little farther each day, some kind of weapon or machine.

"What is it? What is it?" the Ones yelled while they sat paralyzed in front of the Eye. Not many Ones went to work in the factories anymore because they could not stop watching the thing the Others were making. It got longer and longer, until one day, it was out of sight.

This was a very frightening moment, and the Ones screamed at each other. "What are they doing? What kind of weapon is that? Is it aimed at us?"

As they could no longer see the machine that the Others were building, they went back to watching the village of the Others. They steered the Eye along the village, but it seemed that the Others had disappeared from their homes and factories. Eventually, the Ones located the Others. They were all in a circular building on top of their mountain. The Ones maneuvered the Eye so that they could look into the building, where they found the Others sitting in clusters, watching a screen. On the screen of the Others, the Ones were visible. Immediately the Ones understood: the Others were spying on them. They must have seen the Eye and built something similar! The Ones noticed immediately that the Others did not appear friendly; their faces were contorted in disgust, hatred, and fear as they looked at the screen.

"Why must they be so suspicious?" the Ones lamented. "Why do they hate us? We did not do anything, we just looked. Why can't we have kind neighbors who are like us?"

In that instant, the Ones realized that they were too vulnerable up on the mountain. If the Others could see them like that, they were in immediate danger, they could be pointing a weapon at them. In the following weeks, they constructed an underground shelter. The children and the women went in, carrying months' worth of supplies, and a little while later, the men joined them too, carrying weapons that would protect them if the Others dared to attack them underground.

The screen of the Eye was moved so the Ones could watch it from the bunker. They saw the Others running around their village, carrying children, blankets, supplies. Women were crying. Suddenly they all disappeared. The men stayed behind with grim looks on their faces, holding weapons. Then they disappeared as well.

"What are they doing?" the Ones cried in their bunker. "Why are they carrying weapons? Why must they be so aggressive to us?"

They watched the Eye, mesmerized, mortified. For the next few years, the Ones stayed in the underground shelter, going up to the surface only once in a while to gather food and supplies.

Life underground, in a constant state of distress, was not good for the Ones. Disease broke out, as did random violence, while knowledge of how to build and grow things deteriorated. No one was interested in the small worlds of the microscope (the veins of a leaf, or a grain of salt). Instead, they just watched the Others and argued among themselves, because they were so tense and deprived of sleep. And after a decade, or maybe a couple of decades, the Ones perished. All of them.

The smoke in the valley dissipated quickly after the factories stopped working. Rays of sunlight shone through the windows of the deserted houses. The microscopes lay abandoned on the floor, and outside the streets were overgrown by trees and ivy. Stars shone brightly in the clear night sky. And if anyone ever went to the abandoned village of the Ones, they would still find the arm of the Eye that was built on the top of the mountain, extending far, far, far out into the atmosphere, the stratosphere, the cosmos, where it looped around a planet so distant that light traveled days to reach it, before turning back toward the Ones again, where the Eye hung over the village, staring.

The Inverted Gallery

The Curator looked like a curator. He wore black rectangular glasses, a dark turtleneck, and sometimes a thin scarf. It was his choice to look like a curator, so as to not distract from the Art. He had worked at the Gallery in the capital for decades, and everyone knew him simply as the Curator. He also thought of himself as the Curator most of the time, aside from rare moments when he was a Relative around his family, a Patient in a hospital, or a Lover in bed.

The Gallery was the center of his world, and curating was his language for communicating with the Real World outside. He worked every day, often until deep in the night. People projected upon him simplistic notions about "hiding from life" or being a "workaholic," but to him, curating was the fullest expression of his being, of being alive.

The Curator understood and saw things others did not, he noticed deep connections, and he had a sense of the changing needs, fears, and fascinations of people. He tried, through his exhibitions, to show images, narratives, and concepts that reflected upon these changes, that revealed and soothed.

Art, he believed, was needed to continually heal the Real World, even when this healing was disruption, because before healing comes understanding, and before understanding comes revealing, and before revealing comes disruption.

"There is nothing that people need more than to heal," the Curator had said in all earnestness to his partner on the night they first met. "And I want to contribute a tiny bit to that healing."

Now, it was time for a new show.

The Curator stood in his empty gallery. It was his habit to have the Gallery completely empty and closed for two weeks between exhibitions. The Board detested this but agreed to it, because the Curator's attendance numbers were unparalleled.

An empty gallery, a silent space of nothing: this was at once the most frightening and most inspiring thing to the Curator. When he spent several days in an empty gallery, he usually received ideas about what the Real World needed from the Art World at that time. It was as if the walls whispered it to him. In fact, the Curator believed that the walls of the Gallery did whisper to him, but he never talked to anyone about that.

This time, however, no ideas came. The walls remained silent.

The Curator waited two weeks in the Gallery. He then decided to go into the Real World and take the metro. He thought it might help, to go around and around the city on the underground, to encounter the faces of the people, to smell them, to sense their energy. From his seat in the metro the Curator found himself studying the advertising on the walls of the underground. One ad showed an elegant model posing in a sailor costume on a boat. His sailor hat was too white to ever have been at sea, and his pale skin seemed to never have been touched by the sun. It was an ad that did not want to show a sailor, but only the idea of a sailor, a sailor who did not sail but carried the emblems of freedom and nature.

"What is a sailor who does not sail?" the Curator wondered.

Another ad showed a woman in camouflage gear in the city. The green-and-brown camouflage did not hide her but made her stand out among the gray skyscrapers. She was wearing the references to some kind of war mentality.

"What is camouflage that does not camouflage?" the Curator wondered.

The images were telling stories about stories, referring to ideas that were referring to ideas, but no longer linked to their core origin.

He looked at the people around him. Their outfits combined styles from different times with styles from different social groups, without the person wearing them belonging to any of these times or social groups.

He listened to the voices of the people in the train car, the way the young people talked. "I'm in my villain era," one said, while another referred to herself as "matcha girl meets sad summer." The older people spoke in a similar way, referring to themselves as concepts. "You know me, I don't do small. I go big," and "I am someone who needs others to *show up*, you know? That's just who I *am*."

Suddenly he wondered if the Real World was still there. Every part of life seemed to have moved into a narrative. He saw nothing but artifacts, copies, imitations, masks, performances, stories, concepts, mythologies, ideas about ideas, reflections upon reflections, everywhere he looked, but especially with the people themselves. They were living their personas, like actors eaten by their costumes.

The Curator saw his reflection in the dark window of the metro. The Curator outfit, the thin scarf. He could not even grasp the concept of the Real World anymore for a moment. Like a person in a two-dimensional reality would struggle to grasp a three-dimensional one, he too, in a reverse struggle, was not able for a moment to comprehend what it was like to have an authentic, directly lived experience without immediately narrating it. Only for short moments, such as when someone slipped in front of him on the metro stairs and had to rebalance, or when someone lost his temper while trying to board the subway in a rush, did the Curator glimpse the presence of moments free of self-awareness, fragments of the Real World that were still living and breathing beneath the manufactured one, before the performance resumed.

After this trip around the capital, the Curator returned to the Gallery and listened to its silence for one more week. When nothing came to him, the Curator told the Board that the next exhibition was to be postponed. He took a month off to travel to the countryside where he was born. Instead of going to his parents, who always wanted to talk to him about work, he went to his grandmother, who was only barely aware of his job.

In the countryside too the Real World was contaminated. Jam was sold in jars covered with pieces of old-fashioned cloth, which used to be needed as a layer between the jam and the paraffin seal but now was unnecessarily added as a reference to the concept of jam, invoking an old country charm. Billboards had emerged, featuring local politicians posing on tractors in meadows, promising to bring rural life back to how it supposedly once was, with busty white women and no foreigners.

At his grandmother's house the Curator spent three weeks in bed, in crisis, until his grandmother had enough of it. She made him wear one of her flowered aprons and commanded him to weed the garden. Then she ordered him to do some odd jobs and maintenance. The work helped him regain some energy, though he could not help reflecting on the fact that he was continually reflecting on the idea of himself mending the fence. He tried to practice mindfulness exercises, but the idea that he needed this detour to return to himself depressed him and seemed to go against what he was trying to achieve in the first place.

On his last night before he had to return to the Gallery, the Curator watched his grandmother clean her stove, as she did every evening. She did it slowly and deliberately. Never was there a trace of haste to her movements, never a sense of annoyance or enjoyment of the process. She was simply there, cleaning it. She did not know it was a moment that was in any way special; in fact, she did not reflect on her moments in any way. She was entirely free of the idea of herself.

And in that moment, the Curator knew what the next exhibition should be. He asked his grandmother if she'd be willing to come to the capital with him and perform the cleaning of the stove at the Gallery.

At first, she was reluctant. She did not want to leave her hens and her dogs; she did not want to go to the capital, where she did not understand how public transportation worked and where everything made a lot of noise all the time. But the Curator immediately had an intern drive over who claimed to always have dreamed of caring for dogs and hens, who found a quiet hotel room in the city, and who arranged for a car and driver. His grandmother agreed to go, eventually, not because of the hotel and the car, but because she understood it had to do with her grandson's work, and she respected work, even when she did not know what it was for.

The Curator was energized. He had the stove picked up and brought to the Gallery, and his grandmother was housed in the hotel next door. He announced the new exhibition to the Board. He first wanted to call it *In Search of the Authentic*, but the word "authentic" had become so contaminated the Curator had to drink a glass of water each time he uttered the word, so it became *A Moment Without Stories*.

The exhibition was open for only one hour a day, between five and six. He simply put the stove in the central room in the Gallery, placed chairs around it, and put his grandmother in a spotlight in the middle. He had a water tap installed, and there was a bucket, tea towels, and cloths, just like in her home.

The title card on the wall next to the performance read:

> SHE IS HERE, AND SHE CLEANS, FIRST TAKING THE BURNERS FROM THE STOVE AND PUTTING THEM IN A TUB OF SOAPY WATER WHILE CLEANING THE STOVE SURFACE WITH A WET CLOTH. THE BURNERS, AFTER HAVING SOAKED, ARE CLEANED WITH AN IRON SPONGE. THEY ARE DRIED WITH A TEA TOWEL AND LAID OUT ONTO ANOTHER TEA TOWEL, TO LET THE WATER IN THE LITTLE GROOVES OF THE BURNERS DRY. A FINAL TEA TOWEL IS USED TO DRY THE

STOVE. THE KNOBS ARE CLEANED WITH A SEMIDRY CLOTH. THEN THE BURNERS ARE PLACED BACK.

When the show opened, the audience streamed in and sat down, quietly murmuring. The Curator watched his grandmother stand in the spotlight and blink a few times at the audience, looking vaguely helpless. Then she shrugged, opened the tap, and held the bucket under the water stream. She proceeded to soak the burners of the stove.

In the press conference afterward, she answered questions:

Press: How did you feel about cleaning the stove?

Grandmother: *[after a long pause]* I clean my stove at home because I use it. If you don't use it, you can clean it once every two weeks.

Press: What is your feminist perspective on being displayed here cleaning, while it is exactly this stereotype that has been fought for so long?

Grandmother: *[after a long pause]* My husband never cleaned the stove.

This was the headline most papers ran with the next day, in the rave reviews of the show. As the days went by, more news outlets came, and they had various commentators write about her body language, the philosophical connotations of the cleaning, and some intersectional interpretations of her words.

All over the country, replicas of his grandmother's stove were sold, together with books and tutorials on how to clean them. Reviewers said they had found moments of enlightenment and relief from life's heavy weight.

The Curator remained a loyal daily visitor to the five o'clock show. He sat back in his seat and watched his grandmother clean, undisturbed. On the tenth day, his grandmother suddenly stopped cleaning and looked at the audience—straight at the Curator, in fact, although she could not see him because of the blinding lights on her—and started to talk.

"I have to tell you all," she said to the invisible audience, "that if you haven't learned how to clean a stove by now, you will probably never learn it."

It was silent. The people in the audience shuffled around a bit. One person clapped, which caught on, but it did not last. Silence again. The spotlight remained on his grandmother, who moved her weight from one foot to another. The Curator felt like he had to get up and get her, but he stayed pinned to his seat as he watched his grandmother shuffle around on the stage, searching in the audience for the familiar face of her grandson. Then, when no one came to her aid, she looked at the clock.

Thirty minutes left.

She put the cloth down and stepped around the stove, in front of the audience.

"In the war, I stole potatoes for my family," she said. "I worked in a factory. We had to sort the potatoes. Everyone was hungry at the time. I mean the majority of the people at the time were hungry. And if you're going to sort potatoes all day, and you've got nothing to eat, you're going to go home thinking about those potatoes. So I got it into my head to take three small ones, for my three sisters. I sewed a seam into my skirt. It was big enough for three small potatoes. But they caught me. And they fired me in front of everyone."

His grandmother, the Curator realized, in her confusion about what was wanted from her, had started confessing to her sins. Stolen potatoes, a lottery ticket that had gone missing, a kitchen kiss with a brother-in-law that she had neither initiated nor rejected. She continued to confess her measly crimes and imagined transgressions. When she had no more crimes to confess, she stared silently in the distance, her head shaking a little. Then the audience burst out in wild applause. One woman stood up and yelled: "Forgive yourself!" Some people cried and embraced each other. Others called out: "We love you, Grandmother! We learn from you!"

The next night, the Curator nervously sat down in his seat at five o'clock. He noticed the shift in his grandmother as soon as she entered the room, pulling at her skirt, straightening her back. "Here she is," she announced to the audience. And as she cleaned, she addressed the audience in a professional manner, as if she were on a TV show. "Make sure the water is hot but not scalding," she said. "And always make sure to wring out every cloth, because I run a tight ship."

The Curator watched in despair the breaking of his final piece of authenticity. After five minutes, he stood up and went to his grandmother. He thanked her and said she could stop. She was very relieved. The show was closed indefinitely.

That night the Curator went to bed and said to his partner, "I have destroyed the last bit of authenticity I had in my life."

His partner said, "I am sure it's not that bad."

The Curator said, "I no longer believe in Art."

"I am sure that won't last long," his partner said.

And by four a.m. the Curator was up again and walking through his empty dark gallery.

"What now?" he whispered.

He realized there was a flutter of joy in the question.

"What now?" he continued to say. "What now? What now?"

And then, in a daring, tempting way, he yelled: "What now?"

And this time, the Gallery answered him again. It said, "Abandon all old knowledge. This will feel like death. Embrace it."

The Curator opened the doors and the windows of the Gallery, letting the rain and the wind come in. He kicked soil that was in the backyard into the hallway of the gallery, kicking in insects, gravel, and weeds. He beckoned for the raccoon that was rummaging in the bins behind the Gallery's cafeteria and yelled, "Hello, come in," to a homeless man who walked down the dark street in front of the Gallery, though he did not look up.

Finally, he took down the sign that hung above the entrance door, that said THE GALLERY, and hung it on the inside of the door. What used to be the exit of the Gallery now became the entrance to the Gallery. And what used to be the entrance to the Gallery became the entrance to the Real World.

Bette A., the Dutch artist, activist, and author formally known as Bette Adriaanse, writes her stories and novels simultaneously in both Dutch and English. She is the co-founder of the global Heroines! Movement and the co-author of *What Art Does*, with Brian Eno, with whom she collaborates regularly. Bette A.'s novel *Rus, Like Everyone Else* and *What's Mine* are published in North America by Unnamed Press. She lives in Amsterdam.